H.

D0975089

For everyone at Warren Wilson

❖ *Contents*

❖ Leaving by the Window

My father's stories were always told to me in cars: first the Packard, then the Plymouth, then the Studebaker Lark. The cars, like the stories, started out large, extravagant with detail, then narrowed over the years until they were small in scale and scope. We would go for long rides up and down Virginia, sometimes hundreds of miles, beginning in the year my mother died. The motion of the car seemed to hurry his thoughts and he said things at that speed when the country was just a blur beyond the window that he could never say in the stillness of the house.

The news of my mother's death was told to me in a vehicle that would soon become more familiar to me than my own room.

The principal himself came to get me out of class and I knew right away that was a bad sign. He didn't say anything, just took me to the glass doors in front of the school and said, "Your father's here."

His white Studebaker station wagon seemed so small squeezed in between two yellow buses. He leaned over and pushed the door open. I didn't want to get in, would rather have turned around and gone back to Room 203 and listened to Mrs. Baines talk about the Mayans, how they made some sense out of the stars and came up with a calendar they could count on, how they had created a kind of safety and order in their lives when everything around them grew wild.

The radio was turned up loud and Patsy Cline was singing. My father practically had to shout over her. "We're going to the Y."

I turned the radio down. "But there's no water in the pool this time of year," I reminded him.

I wanted him to say something that made perfect sense, to make the day go back to being a regular Wednesday again instead of the kind of day when the world could come undone, but he said, "Well, we're going to see about joining up in the spring."

There was a loose piece of vinyl stripping on the side of my seat. I pulled on it so hard that it opened a seam in the upholstery and I buried my fingers in the soft stuffing.

He pulled into the parking lot by the swimming pool and didn't make a move to get out of the car. We sat there looking at the chain link fence and just beyond it to the gaping blue-green cavity with faded black numbers counting off the depths—3, 4, 8. The lifeguard's chair had a cushion of snow on the seat, and there was snow, too, on the steps of the ladder leading to it. The blue-and-white-striped awning flailed against the metal scaffolding, tearing itself to shreds in the cold January wind.

"Are you brave?" he asked.

I had to answer "Yes." No other answer seemed possible.

"Are you strong?"

I thought about a movie I'd seen, a blindfolded man standing in front of a wall and another man giving the orders to the firing line. The last cigarette took a long, long time. "Ready," and the pause. "Aim . . ."

My jaw clenched and I bit the side of my mouth, hard. My fingers groped in the stuffing until I found something metal to hold onto. I closed my eyes.

"Matty, your mother died last night. Matty, are you listening?"

❖ The funeral happened without me. I was kept away by well-meaning people and when I appealed to my father for intervention he said I should just keep some other picture of her in my mind instead of the one I would get from the cemetery. I stayed at home, restless and angry with a babysitter who didn't know what to say to me. While she watched TV, I slipped out the back door. It had been snowing hard all day, and drifts the size of whales lay beached around the house. I felt like I was floating out to sea, all the landmarks covered up, the sky as white as waves on water. I walked to the edge of the woods behind the house toward the largest drift, a perfect hill of white sculpted by wind. I knelt in front of the dune and started to dig with my hands, scooping out a burrow in its side. When the burrow was big enough I crawled in and lay there, curled, looking out at the black sky that bristled with the light of stars as sharp and cold as broken glass. I waited what seemed hours until I heard my father's car pull in the drive, and then I waited a while longer for him to discover I was gone, to hear my name called out the back door. I was freezing, I couldn't wait any longer. Numb with cold, I climbed out of the burrow and followed my own footprints through the stillness back to the lighted house.

❖ After the funeral it seemed we began to look everywhere for her. He drove me to the place in a distant state where he said I was conceived. We walked around the house, trudging through piles of leaves that had blown against the stone foundation. The curtains were drawn, the screen door hurled itself to meet the door frame over and over again. There was nothing to see. I had no memory of that place at all.

My father was on one side of the house, trying to look into the kitchen, and I was sat on the front porch when a neighbor, looking concerned, shouted across the lawn, "Are you looking for someone in particular?" I turned to see what she was staring at: my father peering into the windows, his old black raincoat with the hem coming down, flapping in the wind.

Once we drove to New York City to find the place in the Village where he first met my mother. It turned out to be a cafe where they made complicated kinds of coffee—espresso, cappuccino, *borgia,* Vienna. We sat there on little iron stools on the sidewalk while my father looked down the street in the direction from which she must have come. I drank my hot chocolate with a long-handled spoon, a sip at a time, to make it last. I pictured my mother, her dark straight hair pulled back with a barrette, just out of college and walking down that sidewalk in the summer heat to meet him. I wanted him to look at me and see her face mixed in with mine. My father's black coffee steamed into the air, untouched, while he gazed fixedly somewhere just over the top of my head.

❖ He was working his way back in time and eventually on one of our journeys we found our way to his hometown, a place that had taken him fifty-seven years to get back to. I was eleven when I first saw it.

He always told me he was born in a place where dreams belonged to the devil. I looked for evidence of this as we drove down the single street of the small town called The Plains, Virginia. The name itself was a dream. The town was hemmed in by hills and thick woods, the long, limitless view blocked. The town that imagined itself being in the midst of something vast was nothing more than a hamlet hunkered down in the lowlands, pinned in the shadow of a stone church that loomed above every other building.

We rolled to a stop in the middle of the street and he pointed to a white clapboard house with a tangle of winter vines crawling up the side. "Wisteria," he explained, but I couldn't envision those heavy purple blooms along the dry, naked vine. He pointed again, to a room that seemed added on to the house, with a low ceiling and sloping roof. "I was born right there in that room!" He said this as if he couldn't quite believe it. I tried to imagine my father as an infant tended by women in that small room, tried to picture his own father nervous and too tall for the shallow hallway, just outside the door.

"This is where it all started." He spoke with a sad amazement in his voice. He turned his hands over as if seeing them for the first time and, finding them too heavy, laid them down and held on to the steering wheel. I felt pulled toward him like a magnet to true north across that vinyl seat, and if either of us had had any practice at all I could have moved up close and he could have put his arm around me, but sadness settled down like a third person between us. The engine idled roughly, nearly stalling more than once as we sat there. I saw a curtain part in an upstairs window, a hand that held it aside to look. I couldn't see a face. After a long time he released the car from neutral and we pulled slowly, almost reluctantly, away.

❖ All that summer we were mostly on the road. He was selling advertising for a magazine that he and my mother had started the year I was born. I don't know whether it was because I had just turned twelve that he began to pay more attention to me, or the fact that my mother was gone and he simply had no one to talk to, but he began to tell me things he hadn't thought about in a long time— about the time when he was fourteen or fifteen and started to feel the town becoming too small, like a coat he'd outgrown. He said he'd been reading poetry—Yeats, Joyce, Rimbaud—and after that, nothing was the same again. He started wandering off, first on short trips by train to Baltimore or Washington for the weekend. Then the trips started getting longer and he found it harder and harder to come home again. He went south and because he didn't have the money he did what the hoboes who befriended him called "riding the rails," made a catwalk out of a plank in the narrow space beneath the box-car and lay on it, inches from the moving ground.

Each time he went farther, stayed longer. He rode the rails to New Orleans and spent a summer in the French Quarter living in a garret and writing poetry. He stood up in front of strangers and read aloud in the Old Absinthe Bar on Bourbon Street.

"I've been there and back, Matty," he'd say, honking the horn for punctuation. You could tell he liked himself a lot then, the kind of life he had. "Intrepid," he'd say with pride, as if the word had been given to him alone, for his motto or his nickname.

I'd get restless just listening to him. My own life seemed colorless and thin in comparison, and I wanted some stories of my own to tell. But I loved being the audience, even when I'd heard all his stories a dozen times. There was a rhythm to all of it, like a wave I could almost give myself to, and even the repetitions comforted me because, for once in my life, I felt with some growing degree of certainty that I knew what was coming.

❖ We were driving into town to get the mail across the Rappahannock Bridge, an old, rusted steel span with a wooden roadbed, when my father stopped the car in the middle. It was a single-lane bridge, and there were no cars coming either way. We just sat there with the windows rolled down and drank our sodas and passed a box of Cheez-it crackers between us. The river was slow and shallow, with willows trailing their branches deep into the water as if they were searching for something. He was not getting over my mother anytime soon and no matter how hard I listened to his stories, I could not reel him back.

"Tell me about the time you drove off the road, how the honeysuckle vines caught you and saved your life," I said, but he was somewhere else. I watched the river flow away from us and the willows that tried to hold it back and I felt him drifting slowly beyond my reach into memories that excluded me, back into a time that stood like a house with many windows, all of which opened onto wider views. In one of those windows, my mother before she was my mother stood, beckoning only to him.

❖ This is my story. I'll tell it only once. I didn't take anything with me except a transistor radio and the thirty-two dollars I'd saved for a guitar. I put these things in my father's small battered leather suitcase which he had given me for my tenth birthday. The brown leather was plastered with decals: Beautiful Florida, Grand Canyon Village,

Sunshine State, Visit Louisiana! When my father gave me the suitcase he said, "I've been there and back!" and I thought he probably should have painted those words right on the case—his very own slogan. The decals were living proof of his journeys. The suitcase wouldn't hold more than a spare shirt and socks, a book or two.

I pulled the small ID tag from its cracked leather holder and it didn't come out easily, stuck to the plastic window by some Florida heat or New Orleans sticky summer night. I pulled it free, finally, and with a pen wrote over the *H* of his initial and made it into the *M* of mine—so easy to make the lines join at a definite point.

I sat down at the desk and spread some newspaper in front of me. I took out the scissors and leaned forward over the paper. I held out a long hank of my hair in one hand and cut it away with the other. I left it there, piled on the paper like a nest of light brown grass. I looked at my reflection in the mirror and was shocked and pleased at how different I looked, how simple it was to change.

I left a note:

> *You always said it was better to travel hopefully than to arrive.*
>
> > *Hopefully,*
> > *Matty*

I left it propped up next to the hair.

I waited until it was good and dark, then I pushed the window open and dropped the suitcase into the grass below. I slid my leg over the sill, then eased the other over, lowering my body with my arms until I could feel the grass brush against the bare soles of my feet. Then I let go and dropped to the ground. I picked up the suitcase and held my shoes in my other hand, then walked to the road.

I turned to look back at the house, the dark window where my father slept not even realizing that I was out there, standing at the end of the yard with his suitcase in my hand, about to walk away. I had a map in my head, compass points clearly marked with all his destinations. I knew which city to head for, which town came next, what state came after that. I'd been a good listener, I'd been to each place at least a dozen times in my mind and could find my way back again. Now it was my turn.

I turned from the house and walked down the road through a tunnel of trees leaning together in the slight wind. The road drew an unwavering black line that cut through the fields of long grass nearly white in the moonlight. Horses, gray shapes grazing on the hill, lifted their heads slowly as I passed and did not stretch their long necks back to earth until I was out of sight.

❖ The bus station was nothing more than a small room in the back of the Texaco station with a bench outside. It was 2:00 A.M. and I'd walked seven miles. I hadn't counted on it being closed. A hand-written sign on the door said to pay the driver the fare. I sat on the bench next to the Coke machine—a red trough with a padlocked lid that rumbled so much I could hear the bottles clinking against each other inside. I took my radio out of the suitcase. I switched it on and listened to a station all the way from Chicago. I waited for the bus to Baltimore, two hours to the north.

My father had told me many times about the port of Sparrows Point near Dundalk just outside Baltimore. At seventeen he convinced the captain of a ship called the *Nora Lee* bound for Belfast that he was really twenty-one and got hired as a mess boy in the galley. Each time he told it I could feel his triumph, his passing for older than he was, his setting out on a voyage to his ancestral home. I could see him sneaking out to the stern as the *Nora Lee* pulled away from Maryland to watch America rise from its shoreline, then fade away into the curve of the earth. I liked to picture him leaning against the railing after the night's dinner was cooked, smoking a cigarette and tilting his head back to see the stars. He wouldn't have known any constellations or been able to distinguish the steady glow of a planet from the rest, but he would have stayed a long time in the wind and dark, with the tent of his father's coat pulled close around him.

❖ I didn't have to wait long. The bus came down Main Street, its turn signal flashing orange as it swung into the station parking lot. The door opened with a hiss, and the driver, an enormous man who seemed to spill over his seat, flicked on a small light and took out a receipt book of tickets. He wore a change maker as silver and intricate as a flute strapped onto a thick leather belt. Folds of flesh overlapped it and he had to sit up straight to get his thumb on the levers.

"Where you goin' this time of night?" he asked.

With a tone as dead certain as I could manage I said, "Baltimore. Give me a ticket through to Baltimore."

He looked hard at me and I stared him back like I knew where I was going, even turned the suitcase a little so he could see the stickers and held it like a shield in front of me.

"That'll be two dollars and seventy-five cents," he said, and his thumb bore down on the lever that released a quarter into his thick fingers, one of them cinched tight with a ring that would have to be cut to ever come off again.

With another hiss of escaping air the doors folded shut and sealed us in. I made my way to the back where I could sit with my feet propped up on the wheel well. There were only three other people on the bus and they were all sleeping with their heads rolled back, mouths open. I brushed past a sailor with his white cap pulled down like a shade.

Near the back, a thin, reedy-looking woman in a pink dress held a small boy, limp as a towel, across her narrow lap. He had his thumb in his mouth and when I sat down across from them he sucked hard on it for a minute. Then his mouth grew slack again.

I was wide awake, even after the long walk. The bus was grinding through so many gears getting up to speed I lost track of the number. I watched the lights of town streaking back, as if the whole place were pulling away from its moorings, carried on a current out to sea. The last thing to go was the A&P parking lot where my father let me drive the car early one Sunday morning. He held on to the door handle the whole time as I slalomed around the light poles and crisscrossed the endless rows of empty parking spaces again and again as if each pass could erase a little more of those careful white lines.

❖ Baltimore was red with sunrise and brick row houses. Metal chairs waited on the porches, lights flashed on behind windows. It seemed strange to me, people living side by side like that, able to see inside each other's houses with a casual glance.

It was not a clean city, and the deeper we drove into it the uglier it got. Newspapers blew across vacant lots and stuck to the chain link fencing. When we stopped at a light I saw a man pissing against a wall, a dark pool spread into the dust at his feet. At the next light there was a woman, her bare arms the color of piecrust dough sitting on a stoop smoking a cigarette with one hand, holding on to a baby with the other. During the two long minutes from red to green she watched the smoke drift slowly in the still air. She never once looked at the baby.

The bus lurched into the station. Everyone staggered to their feet, groping in the overhead bins for their belongings.

The driver was writing something on a clipboard as I passed him. "Watch your step," he said without looking up. "And watch your back, too." I looked quickly behind me. He shook his head and his body jiggled as he laughed. "No, sugar, out there." His forefinger poked at the air and pointed to the world outside the bus. His thumb flipped the change meter four times and he took my hand and poured a stream of quarters into it. "Refund. Get yourself some breakfast. You'll be needing it."

❖ I sat down at the counter and ordered some cornflakes. A boy in a raincoat sat two stools away twirling a spoon around in an empty cup of coffee. We kept looking at each other in the mirror behind the counter. I watched his reflection move toward me and sit on the stool next to me. He had pale skin and dark crescent moons under his eyes. We stared at each other in the mirror on the opposite wall. He looked down and I followed his eyes to my suit-case.

"You been to all those places?"

"Some."

"You leaving home? You don't look old enough to just be on vaca-tion."

I shrugged. He didn't wait for an answer but went on.

"This is my third time out. They don't even try to look for me anymore."

His name was Luke. He said he was sixteen. "From New Hope, where there isn't any."

Maybe he was telling the truth, maybe not. But I felt like I could call myself anything I wanted, try out a new age, be from somewhere else. So I told him my name was Luz, after a Spanish girl I liked in school. Luke didn't know any Spanish and heard the word as Luce —"Short for Lucy, right?"—and I didn't try to tell him any differ-ent. I also said I was fifteen and from Paris, Virginia, which was just a place where my father and I stayed in a motel once, but a place I liked the sound of.

"You got anyplace in mind to go to?" he asked my face in the mirror.

"Sparrows Point," I told him. "It's a port somewhere near here."

"It's a nice name, what the hell," he said.

We went to find an information booth to see about getting anoth-er bus and for a minute I felt scared, wondering if maybe my father made this place up like I just picked myself another name. Maybe there was no way to follow him, maybe it was all a lie, a false trail zigzagging around a secret life.

"Dundalk bus is at Gate 6, stops at Sparrows Point," Luke said, his finger pressing against the word halfway down the posted sched-ule, underlining its simple truth with his bitten nail.

❖ Dundalk was not the misty, green place on the Irish coast for which it was named but a smog-gray and grimy port bristling with cranes on the Patapsco River. I felt sick with a growing disappointment I couldn't fully admit to yet. The adrenalin that kept me going all night suddenly left me feeling empty and hungry and thin. But this was just Dundalk and I told myself Sparrows Point would be a better place. Even its name sounded promising.

The bus continued on to a much smaller port. A single ship, unloaded, with all its watermarks showing like the hem of a slip, was tethered to the pier. The bus let us out in front of a place called the Streamliner Diner that flared silver in the sun. We went in and sat down in a red vinyl booth.

"Sonofabitch left me a nickel tip!" the waitress shouted to nobody in particular from the next booth where she swiped at the formica with a greasy towel. The name "Nan" was stitched in shaky writing across her breast pocket. Her hair was a color I couldn't find a word for, somewhere between gray and red and blond. She piled two plates still sticky with syrup and egg yolk on top of one another, then dumped a full ashtray onto the top plate. With the other hand she wadded up paper placemats with maps of Maryland on them.

"What'll you two have?" The waitress thumbed through her order pad and didn't even look at us.

"Bacon and eggs, over easy, and a side of grits with extra butter," Luke said.

"I'll have the same." I said this as if I'd ordered it a hundred times when I'd never eaten an egg in my life that wasn't scrambled. But it seemed like everything ought to change somehow, especially since I was somebody else already and had not slept in my bed the night before.

For the first time I thought of my father walking into my empty room, picking up the note. I watched him as he touched my hair on the paper and felt the stricture in his chest as he saw the open window and realized how like him I'd become.

❖ We spent the day sitting by the water mostly waiting for the night.

"Are your folks looking for you?" Luke asked.

"Just my father."

"Not your mother too?"

"I don't have a mother anymore."

"Is she dead, or just gone?"

"Both."

A tug escorted by a flock of seagulls pushed an empty barge toward the open bay. The engine throbbed, its steady strokes reverberating off the water's flat surface like the stretched skin of a drum. I watched it go until it was just a speck on the water, a black tail of blurred smoke trailing behind.

"But would she look for you if she was alive?" He seemed intent on finding out, as if he'd never met anyone who'd been missed enough to be searched for.

Would she? "Sure," I told him. To myself, I honestly couldn't say. It was so hard to imagine her doing anything anymore.

❖ Night came on slowly and the dark blue seeped down into the yellow horizon the way ink blends into water. Lights of the ship flashed on; a constellation gradually revealed itself. We watched the crew come down the ramp for dinner, laughing and jostling each other through the door into the diner.

We stood close to the ship without a clue as to how to get on it or where to go once we did. The beam of a flashlight cut through the dark above the deck. We couldn't see the hand that held it. The beam swept in a long arc toward us as if it knew we were there and sliced through us as easily as the blade of a magician's saw. We stood, frozen, transfixed as deer in the sudden light. Someone at the other end of the light hollered and we ran for the tall marsh grass behind us.

The marsh sucked at our shoes, and cattails slapped against us as we ran. Gradually the ground got firmer, the grass tapered down, and we came up an embankment to a railroad track. The sharp smell of creosote hung in the air. Luke put his ear down on the rail, which shone like a blade in the light from the rising moon, and listened for the vibration of an engine down the line. I knelt there too, my ear against the cold steel, and far off, I could feel more than hear it— long before the light flared down the tracks—the train coming. I put a penny down, out of habit, then we backed away over the edge of the bank and lay next to each other. The rails quivered with the weight of at least a hundred wheels.

"You have to jump high, grab a rung with at least one hand to get on," Luke shouted above the blast of the whistle. "Leave the suit- case here."

I looked at it lying in the grass, the smooth decals faintly glossed with light. I dug my fingers into the ground, poised like a runner, my body a spring, glad to have simple instructions to follow. But the train was too far from any junction or crossing that could have slowed it down and we watched it pass—wheels and streaks of space between wheels and a sound we couldn't even scream over anymore. Then it was gone, trailing a red light behind. We watched it disappear into a tunnel or around a bend and heard the far-off sound of a crossing bell ringing its tinny warning down the tracks.

I pictured the black-and-white-striped arms lowering down, the red flashing eye in the black, staring socket, and remembered a time in the car with my father. I was in the backseat because my mother was still alive. The bell was clanging, the train coming, the arms low- ering down, and instead of stopping, he made a run for it to get through before it closed. I heard the thud on the roof of the car as the rail came down, heard the splintered crack as we broke its arm, heard my mother's voice rising in anger, "Now why, why on earth did you do that?" My father didn't answer and the train thundered behind us, the first danger we had brushed up against. Unlike my mother, I was not afraid but felt a strange, unholy thrill at his hav- ing taken such a risk and come away unharmed.

❖ When I woke it was not really light yet. I looked up and the sky was a watery blue, a star—Venus probably—burned as bright as the point of paper under a magnifying glass just before it turns to fire.

Luke and I were wrapped around each other, though I didn't remember how we got that way, that motion in the dark toward the warmth of another. The grass, a foot high around the place we'd flattened with our bodies, was bent over with the weight of dew. We stood up, shivering, and looked behind us to the diner down the hill, its red and white sign just coming on, flickering, uncertain at first, then holding steady. Behind it, we could see the empty place on the water where the ship had been.

Luke turned away from the water. "New York, that's the place. More ships—this is a low-class port, just freighters. In New York they've got ocean liners."

I remembered my father telling me about sailing on the maiden voyage of the *Queen Mary* from New York to Southampton, much later than his first voyage. He had money then, and a job waiting for him at the other end.

We headed on foot in the general direction of New York, and it wasn't long before we found a highway. We didn't stand there any longer than fifteen minutes with our thumbs out before a truck stopped and we climbed up on the wheel. Luke pulled me into the cab after him. The driver didn't look that much older than Luke— red hair in a crew cut, aviator sunglasses, a tattoo of a mermaid swimming on his bicep as he shifted the gears.

"I'm headed for Queens," he shouted above the straining engine.

"Is that near New York City?" I asked.

"Close enough."

Queens, *Queen Mary*—it all seemed related.

"Eighteen of these," he said proudly as he shifted. "That's why it's such a drag to stop once you get rolling. You're lucky I did, but hey, I could use the company. I just did three days from L.A. alone, just me and my white crosses." He paused to take a breath. "God-damn," he said, as if after three thousand miles he still couldn't comprehend how he'd gotten there.

We came into Brooklyn by the Verrazano Bridge and soon Brooklyn was gone and we were in Queens, though we crossed no border that I could see. It was late afternoon when he let us off near the East River. He saluted us and grinned, then hauled through at least four of the eighteen gears before he turned a corner and moved out of sight.

We stood on the cobblestone street. A soupy kind of breeze floated in off the river, scented with garbage and brine. We walked in that direction. There were people out on stoops because it was so hot, kids leaping like marionettes in the plumes of water gushing from open hydrants.

We bought some hot dogs from a vendor with a shiny silver cart that sprouted a red and yellow umbrella. He painted them with catsup and mustard.

"The works?" he asked and we watched the dogs disappear under a hill of onions and relish. When he handed me my change I asked him, "Is the *Queen Mary* around here?"

He laughed. "Where you been, Timbuktu? She sailed for the scrap heap a long time ago. Why, you maybe got a ticket?"

He laughed so hard he went into a sneezing fit. I counted nine as we walked away.

Suddenly I felt so tired I didn't think I could move another step. Queens stretched out in too many directions and I wanted to be out to sea, rocked by waves on the long voyage. I wanted, after the crossing, to smell land, the sweet smoke and earth of Ireland where my father said our people came from, and walk ashore to a place that would know my name.

As we got closer to the river, its scent grew stronger, and we came out of the canyons of red brick warehouses into the glaring light on the East River. It was a body of water as silver and thick as mercury, heavy and waveless, with ships ploughing through it toward the white glare of the open harbor.

The ships in port were not liners strung with small colored flags. There were no crowds of people leaning from the deck flinging handfuls of pink confetti onto the heads of the people who waved below. The ship we wanted was sideways, chained to the iron teeth of the dock, the word *Galway* in faded letters across its stern. Cranes were swinging crates as big as houses, and we stood there in the shade of it, watching the loading. I tried to imagine a place inside that hollow, ringing steel that could hide us.

I heard a sound I had only heard once before in my life, in a circus: a wild, trumpeting call. It was an elephant, led backward from a truck down a wooden ramp. It stood on the asphalt, shivering with terror, while two men looped a cloth cinch as big as a sheet beneath its belly. A large hook was threaded through the grommets at the top and the crane's engine roared with the sound a Ferris wheel makes when it starts up. The cable grew taut and the elephant rolled its eyes back. As the cable pulled up, the elephant seemed to stretch its legs down, to keep them planted firmly on the ground. With a jerk, the crane pulled hard and the elephant's feet left the earth, its knees buckling slightly while the legs, as sturdy as trees on the ground, swung helplessly, testing the terrifying emptiness around them. Its trunk lifted, and the animal let out a sound that should have stopped the world. But the crane swung its steel arm over the deck and the elephant disappeared deep inside the hold where it continued to call, the sound echoing mournfully off the steel hull until it sounded like the ship itself was crying out in terror. I thought about what would happen at the other end, and all I could see was the elephant, swinging, a weary shape in the gray, indefinite air of Ireland, coming down onto a terrain that once again would not be home.

❖ There was no way I could turn back now. I was convinced that if I just got on the ship it would be all right, but for the first time I couldn't picture what might happen when I got to Ireland. My father had never made it to Dublin, though that is where he wanted to go— his story trailed off somewhere in Belfast. Did he even get off the ship when it docked?

It was dark and very quiet when we made our move. We had loaded the suitcase with as many provisions as it would hold: candy bars, cans of root beer, oranges. We thought it would be enough to tide us over, though neither of us could guess how long the voyage might be. It would have to be enough. We were out of money.

Luke's knowledge ended at the foot of the gangway and neither of us knew what to expect from there on in. We crouched low and started to crawl along the wooden ramp. I grabbed on to a corner of his jacket and held the suitcase tight against my chest. We were almost to the deck when a voice behind us said, "Well now." Light crawled over our bodies from the man's flashlight. "Going somewhere?" The voice was husky, slow. The man had a lot of time. I could hear him strike a match, draw on a cigarette, let the smoke out in a satisfied way.

"Tell you what." He exhaled again. I could smell it now and it stung my nose. "I won't call the cops." I halfway turned around, but couldn't see his face, just the glaring disk of light and his vague shape behind it. "You kids don't want to be on this floating zoo anyhow. There'll be another ship along tomorrow—I can help you get on if you still want to go . . . You look like you could use a meal, a bath maybe. I got a house in Jersey. You can sleep there."

He turned off the light and then I could see him more clearly. Gray hair and glasses. A man about my father's age.

"Come on—my shift is up. You kids look beat. Car's right across the street." He took the suitcase from me. "How old are you?"

"Fifteen," I lied.

"You?" he said, nodding at Luke.

"Sixteen."

He seemed pleased with our answers.

We walked across the empty loading dock. The crane was silent. The elephant was silent. We walked toward the man's car, a red and white Oldsmobile, a sleek thing crouched in the dark. The man unlocked it, held the door open. I looked at Luke for some signal to break and run, some corroboration of the vague uneasiness

I was feeling trying to guess if the man's words hid something he wasn't saying, but Luke slid across the seat, so I slid in next to him.

"I went to Atlantic City once—always wanted to go back," Luke said to him.

"I live in Newark. No ocean there." He jabbed the key into the lock. The automatic transmission clicked into a single, simple gear called Drive and we headed west across the Hudson.

❖ There was a yard with trees, borders of white flowers. The door opened easily to his key. He set my suitcase down in the hallway. On a narrow table where he set down his keys there was a picture of a girl with dark wings of hair around a heart-shaped face, younger than me. There was a dog, a gray poodle, happy to be touched and fed.

He turned the radio on. He told us to sit at the table while he got us something to eat. Cold chicken, potato salad from a plastic bowl with daisies on it. Lemonade in jelly jar glasses. We waited for him to sit down before we ate. And then we tried to eat as if we had all the time in the world.

He took me upstairs after dinner. "Here's a clean towel," he said. "You can take your bath now."

I closed the door behind me. I turned on the water and the tub filled fast. I got in, submerged myself up to my chin and leaned back, my head resting on the hard, curved arm of the porcelain tub. I closed my eyes.

The door opened, then closed again. I didn't want to open my eyes.

"Stand up," he said. "I want to see what you look like."

At first I didn't move, then I rose slowly out of the water, pulled by a command that I hadn't figured out how to refuse, afraid, too, of what would happen if I didn't do as he told me.

I stood there dripping. I looked at the wall behind him, purple violets and green leaves on pale pink paper. It was peeling away from the wall around the light switch like sunburned skin. Don't look at me, I thought. As long as I didn't look at him I felt I couldn't really be seen.

"Beauty mark," he said, and smiled.

But I had no beauty mark. The door opened, then clicked shut. He was gone. I sank slowly down into the warm water again. And then I noticed something—a dark spot on my stomach. I touched it with the tip of my finger. It was stuck tight, didn't move. A tick. It must have gotten inside my shirt when we slept in the field. I shuddered but I left it there. I smiled to think how I fooled him, I thought it could protect me like a charm, that he wouldn't touch me if he saw it up close, if he found out that what he thought was a mark of beauty was in fact a terrible flaw.

❖ When I came back downstairs to find Luke and tell him what happened he was sitting on the couch with a girl who looked at least sixteen. They were both laughing and drinking red wine out of a bottle, passing it back and forth. The man sat in a chair, his face flushed red with the wine, watching them.

"This is Caroline, my neighbor. Used to be my baby-sitter when my daughter was little."

Caroline barely nodded in my direction. She kicked off her shoes and propped her feet on the coffee table, nearly knocking over a green metal ashtray full of crushed white filters and gray ash.

"Lou," she said to him. "Lou, give the lady a drink. You can't come to the party if you don't have a drink." She twisted her long black hair around her index finger repeatedly as if she were teaching it to curl and it was slow learning.

The man poured me a glass of sweet wine. I tried to catch Luke's eye, but Luke raised the bottle in the air and grinned. "Down the hatch, Luz."

I just stared at him, and then remembered Luz was the name I'd picked for myself. Suddenly I wanted to tell him my real name, and I almost did, but it seemed the only thing I could keep to myself anymore.

"You have to drink it all," the man said to me as if he were telling a child to clean her plate or she couldn't get up from the table.

I drank the glass dry. Whatever happened here would happen to Luz, not to me.

I sat down on the floor and leaned against the coffee table and closed my eyes. I felt like I was swimming, like I did the summer my mother taught me the breaststroke. She taught me to swim all the way out to the raft on the lake where we used to live. She would dive cleanly into the water from the dock and I would smack the water with my belly as I followed. "Truly graceful, Matty," she said as she backstroked away from me. She stood on the raft, dripping, hands on her narrow hips as I struggled with the last fifty yards. She was shouting some instructions to me but I couldn't hear above my own splashing. She reached her hand toward me as I came alongside, gasping for air, and pulled me up to the light and the sun-warmed planks. We lay there face up for a time listening to the soft slap of water against the oil-drum pontoons. Her breathing grew deeper, rhythmical, and soon she was asleep. She "went under," as she would call it, and I pictured her in the green water below, diving toward a deeper green where the water lilies attached their long swaying cords to the silted bottom. I felt protective of her, as if my vigilance while she swam alone through that other world could be a homing signal she would return to, helping her ascend slowly toward the bright surface and break through into the warm, sweet air.

When I opened my eyes, Luke and Caroline were gone and the man was leaning over me.

"Come on, Luce, I've got something to show you."

I shook my head, then before I knew what was happening he reached out, grabbed what little hair was left at the back of my neck and pulled it hard. He yanked my arm and hauled me up the stairs. I concentrated on being too heavy to move, to send down roots into the floor. But still I moved. At the top of the stairs he pushed a door open and thrust me into the room.

"Take a good look."

At first all I could see was an aquarium and the darting, shadowy shapes of angelfish threading through bubbles that rose from a tiny figure of a man in a diving bell. Behind the aquarium something moved and as my eyes grew accustomed to the dark I saw Luke and Caroline, their skin green in the watery light, their bodies heaving with a rhythm I only partly understood.

He twisted my arm behind my back until I thought it would surely break.

"That's what I'm going to do to you," he said, his breath hot and sour in my face.

He shoved me into the hallway and into a dark room. I fell back against a bed. I found my voice and yelled, but it was a thin shield that couldn't stop anything from getting through. I thought of the elephant being lowered screaming into the dark hold of the ship. I took myself there, knee deep in straw, with my hand on the elephant's leathery skin to soothe her as the engine's violent tremors shook through the hull, as the land dropped away and water went from blue to black beneath us.

❖ A gray light seeped into the room. I woke up alone. There was a single drop of blood on the white sheet I couldn't believe came from me. I yanked the covers over it, embarrassed like the day two months ago when I'd worn my coat all day in a hot classroom to hide the sudden evidence of my first menstrual flow, indelibly red on the back of my white wool skirt.

I got up slowly, crawled on the floor to find my clothes. I listened, my ear to the door. The house was utterly still. Luke was somewhere down the hall, asleep with Caroline, and it made me feel sick to think of it. The man had slept in some other room, or on the couch downstairs. I looked around me. White ruffled curtains, a pile of stuffed animals on a window seat. On the dresser, a blue jewelry box. I opened it and a ballerina spun silently on a mirror, whatever music that had once moved her broken inside the music box. I closed the lid. I opened it again. Again the noiseless dance. A slender silver bracelet with a turquoise heart set in its center lay in a velvet compartment all by itself. I tried it on. It fit. I didn't put it back.

The window was hard to open, the frame swollen by household heat and winter cold, but it moved when I pushed my whole weight upward. I climbed out onto the eaves, then crawled a few feet forward to a tree that grew so close to the house it seemed the house was resting against it. I noticed small bits of wood nailed to the trunk—a crude ladder to the ground. I wondered about the man's daughter—had she left this way too?

Once on the ground I broke into a wild run down the tree-lined street until I came to the first intersection. I stuck out my thumb. I only had one thought left—to get back to Sparrows Point, to start over, to get it right this time.

A girl in a sports car picked me up and the Beatles were turned up loud on the radio singing "Love Me Do." Her hair was wound around pink curlers, a yellow scarf tied over it all.

"Cuttin' school?"

I nodded. She smiled.

"I used to do that so much they finally told me to stay home for good. But I showed them—I got a job as a teller at the bank and saved up till I got this car."

I was so relieved I could have cried—there she was talking to me as if I was just a normal person. I drank in all the bright details of her as if I had a sudden, unslakable thirst and she had just handed me a dipper full of water.

"I'm going to Philly," she said, "to see my boyfriend."

"I have to go to Baltimore." I was afraid she would ask me why, but she just grinned at me.

"Sorry I can't get you all the way there, but it's a start anyway."

She handed me a sack of sugared donuts and passed me a bottle of Coke she had wedged between the bucket seats.

She took the ticket at the tollgate to the turnpike and I leaned my head back in the seat and fell asleep as she sang along with the radio.

She woke me at a rest stop. "I get off just up ahead—you can find a ride here, no problem. Good luck to you!"

She roared off, then waved her hand out the window as she looked into her rearview mirror.

I hadn't stood there two minutes when a highway patrol car pulled up next to me.

"Which car here belongs to you?" he asked.

I shrugged.

"Thought so. You'll have to come with me." He opened the back door. A wire grill separated the front seat from the back. I took the silver bracelet off my wrist and jammed it behind the seat, afraid I might be arrested for stealing.

He took me to a precinct and put me in a cell. There was an iron bed without a mattress or a blanket. Someone brought me a cup of coffee and a hamburger. Someone said, "Matty, we've called your father." They knew exactly who I was. The thing is, when the police-woman escorted me to the bathroom and I looked into the mirror above the rusted, dripping sink, I really didn't recognize myself any-more.

"We'll check you, you know," she said with a confident sneer. "We'll have a doctor find out if you did anything—you know what I mean."

Suddenly I was terrified. I didn't want anyone to know, didn't want that part to ruin my story, and was afraid my own body would finally betray me, would break the silence I had to keep.

❖ The radio was on all night long. I couldn't imagine what was taking my father so long unless he thought he was teaching me a lesson by making me spend the night in jail. The cops came in with prostitutes at three in the morning. They all had long legs and lots of teased hair—blond or jet black, never brown. The lights stayed on, neon buzzing in the tubes like flies trapped in a jar. There was no such thing as privacy. If you asked for anything the cops said, "What do you think this is, the Hilton Hotel?" It was their standard joke. They wanted to remind you every minute that you were in their hands.

❖ I thought about my father getting in the car, revving the engine too much to warm it, backing out of the driveway and nearly hitting the gatepost. He knocked it down once. For months there was a pile of white bricks at the edge of the driveway. Grass grew up between them, snow covered the whole mess, and the grass returned once more before he got around to hiring someone to build it back the way it was.

I thought about my father driving the interstate, which he'd always avoided, peering at the unfamiliar green signs, looking at a scribbled note on the seat beside him where I was not sitting to remind him, as I always did, of the right turn to make, when it looked safe to pass. He was traveling on my road now—six lanes of traffic along the eastern seaboard. Trucks were bearing down on him, riding his tail and pulling sharply around and ahead of him. I felt his fear, his awkwardness in coming such a distance to find me.

❖ The cell was unlocked with a key that fit all the other locks on all the other cells. A policeman steered me by the elbow to a room with a single chair in it. "Wait here" was all he said.

I slouched in the chair and looked at my hands, noticed how dirty my fingernails were, how my sneakers looked like I'd lived in them for years. I heard voices coming through the open door from the next room. One voice was my father's but I couldn't hear the words he was saying.

The sergeant came and got me and led me into another room. I saw my father across that room, a man smaller than I remembered —older, too. Neither of us moved toward the other.

I looked away from him, at the light coming through the window, how it made a yellow, fractured rectangle on the floor as it squeezed through the half-open blinds. I waited, frozen to a spot on the floor. Then I looked at him. We faced each other, my

father and I, across that room as if a quicksand mire lay in between.

My father rose unsteadily from the chair. He stood there, hands
at his sides, fingers opening and closing, opening and closing.

"Oh, Matty," he said, not much above a whisper, more to himself than to me.

❖ We didn't speak as we walked to the car. I kept waiting for him to
say something, but for once, he seemed at a complete loss for words.
He opened the door and I slid into the passenger seat. My father
pumped the accelerator and the engine turned over, sluggish, the bat-
tery nearly drained because he'd left the lights on. But it started on the
second try and he steered slowly, cautiously out of the parking lot into
the crowded street. It was dusk, but light enough still to see his face—
a gray mask that revealed nothing of what he was thinking. I watched
the row houses, the lights of their kitchens and the outlines of women
moving through them. There were vacant lots with kids playing stick-
ball, lifting their heads when someone called them home to dinner.

The highway was dark in the long stretches between exits. I cleared
my throat, but let another exit go by before I opened my mouth. I
started to tell him my story. I told him about Sparrows Point, the
ship, except I told about the elephant then instead of the place it
really was. I thought that since it was my story I could tell it like I
wanted. I tried to tell it like the adventure I had in mind. He listened,
both hands on the wheel for once because he wasn't doing the talking. He was paying attention now. Words were spilling from me and
I couldn't stop. I told about the diner, about eating fried eggs, about
the truck and the train. I left Luke out of it because I didn't want him
there, and when I got to the part about Queens and New Jersey and
all that happened there, the words trickled down to nothing. And
then I just stopped talking.

It grew completely dark. Our hands and knees were lit by the green
glow of the dashboard dials, our expressions diffused in underwater
light.

We paid the toll and drove over the long span of the Delaware Bridge. There was a ship below, heading out of the mouth of the river into the black Atlantic, away from the lights of the bridge, the town below. Any other time the sight of a ship would bring on the story of the *Nora Lee*. This time he let it go as if he knew what words could set in motion. Now we both had stories we couldn't tell.

We crossed the state of Maryland without a single word. And still a hundred miles from home I felt my father begin to veer away from me as if in that narrow space and silence we might somehow collide.

I leaned my face against the window. There was a moon and I could see the familiar landmarks of the Blue Ridge Mountains slowly rise to meet us in the distance, the Potomac River running toward the Shenandoah to Harpers Ferry where they would soon converge. The words were gone so soon, the story good for just a single telling. Then I began to feel the heat of my own breath, see the evidence of it on the window, and I made it bloom again and again on the mirrored glass.

❖ *Turnaround*

There is a photograph I keep above my desk in the garage apartment where I live alone now. It's a snapshot a stranger took of us— my ex-wife Susan, my two-year-old son Jonas, and I—and we all smiled when the man told us to, as if we'd known him all our lives. In this picture we're all squinting into the August sun, our arms and legs are sugared with Delaware sand. My arm is around Susan, and Jonas sits between my knees, a plastic shovel clutched in his fist like a scepter. I look at this picture, four years in its frame, a still life of a family that broke apart a month after it was taken. I try to look for some foreshadowing. Susan's wrinkled brow seems not just from the sun's glare, but from a flagrant wariness—hadn't it always been there? In my own face, wasn't there something in that slightly skewed grin that knew I was about to screw up in some unforgivable way? What happened not ten minutes after the photo was taken must have been the very thing she needed, and I've often thought I gave that half minute of negligence to her as an inevitable gift, a reason, finally, that would corroborate her worst fears and my own. No surprise, really. I was still the black sheep of any family I belonged to.

That day Jonas and I played at the water's edge while Susan lay beneath the umbrella and I swear I only got distracted for a minute—closed my eyes and leaned back—then I heard Susan screaming "Jonas!" I sat bolt upright, then pitched myself forward. I hit the waves running, sloppy with fear, searching for his head above the water. Then I went under and I found him. He was a blurred shape in front of me and I reached out and grabbed on to him. His hands were as slippery as fish in my own—and then I lost my balance and the undertow pulled him away. Salt stung my eyes, sand cracked between my teeth. I plunged forward again. I felt but could not see him. I held on tight to his foot and pulled him to me. Once we were on the shore I laid him down and pushed the water from his lungs. He coughed and spit up salt water and cried like he was being born all over again. Then he howled for his mother who lifted him away. I sat there a short distance from them as Susan wrapped him in a pink beach towel. A sand crab crawled on my foot and I didn't have the energy to brush it away. Susan could hardly bring herself to look at me. A line formed, as definite that day as if someone had dragged a stick in the sand between us.

In the days that followed we rarely spoke. I started to eat as if my hunger was a new idea I couldn't stop thinking of. Susan watched me get fat with uncensored disgust. I felt too guilty to protest. All I could think of was how I'd left a mark, not at all in the way a father wants to give something of himself to his son, to his family. Susan would never forget this, I was sure, and Jonas—who knows what he would remember—my hands letting go of him, the terrible feel of the water in his nose, the grip of the undertow raking him out to sea?

I exiled myself to Montana when the divorce became final less than a year later. I chose Montana because it was a landlocked state that, despite its best efforts, could not seem to prosper—its population was actually waning instead of steadily swelling like warmer places. I set my sights as low as possible—I dropped out of medical school, became a directory assistance operator. I lived on next to nothing. I took night classes at the university in art history and anthropology and psychology. I must have looked at women with a longing that pushed them from me before I even said a word. I never approached any of them. I got rid of the demands in my life one at a time.

❖ I look out the window by my desk, at the family that lives in the front house filling up their plastic swimming pool. Their two children bob in the water, buoyant as corks, while their parents sit in their lounge chairs with their sunglasses on, reading magazines, looking up every so often, calmly, as one or the other of their children shouts "Watch me! Watch me!" from the bright blue pool.

❖ When Jonas was a baby I wouldn't carry him. I was terrified I'd drop him or bang his head on some sharp edge of furniture. But as he got older, survived falls from high chairs and swing sets, I thought he had his own good luck that I could no longer ruin.

A month ago I was sitting in a diner in Gary, Indiana, an hour after my father's funeral. It was a diner he used to take me to on Saturday mornings. I sat there at the counter, a grown man with my feet finally reaching the floor, still wanting to order the cornflakes in the little box the way I used to. I could almost hear the sound of his spoon stirring the two lumps of sugar into his coffee long after it had dissolved. We would sit without talking. He never had much to say to me, but he took me places—the mill where he worked all his life, the hardware store whose owner he'd gone to school with, the diner where he liked to spend his Saturday mornings—places where men talked about their luck or lack of it, places where I always seemed to stand just outside their rough circle, listening.

It struck me as I sat there in that diner that I was the same age as my father had been then, and I looked at my hands wrapped around the thick white mug of coffee before me, stirred two spoonfuls of sugar into it though I never took my coffee sweet, and began to cry. I knocked the cup of coffee over. The waitress pushed some extra napkins at me. I guess she was used to people crying, the diner being only a block from the cemetery and customers coming in with damp clots of earth still on their shoes, sitting slouched in the various postures of grief that left them silent, picking at the food they thought they wanted and couldn't eat.

"Forgive me," I said.

"You're forgiven," she answered and wiped the counter.

For a moment it seemed as simple as that—that the woman behind the counter refilling my coffee cup could, out of the blue, absolve me, say something I'd waited my whole life to hear. But there was no way for me to tell her this. I started laughing, couldn't stop myself. Maybe she thought I was hysterical—I'm sure she saw plenty of that too—but I felt broken open and surprised that there was still something silly alive in me after all that fear and sadness.

I thought of Jonas and wished he was there on the stool next to me flipping through the jukebox selections on the counter. Wished that we could be in collusion over some mundane, ridiculous thing like making up an exotic occupation for the man at the end of the counter who wore a tuxedo and had a gym bag on the floor next to his shiny black shoes. Would Jonas have guessed a spy? An undertaker training for the Olympics? I had no idea what Jonas would think about anything.

I called Susan right then from the pay phone next to the coatrack and high chairs. She didn't seem surprised to hear from me and in a conversation that lasted a few minutes I arranged something that had taken me five years to work up to.

❖ As my plane came down over the bay, nearly touching the water with its wheels before it found the runway, I thought of Jonas coming to meet me. He had insisted on taking the bus from Salt Lake City (Susan said he hated planes). At that hour he was most likely coming down the west side of the Sierra and I wondered if we'd intersected briefly en route, my plane throwing a shadow on the white roof of the Greyhound somewhere in Nevada.

I dropped my luggage off at the hotel, then got directions to the bus station. I decided to walk to Seventh Street to meet him, hoping the exercise would tire me. I hadn't slept well in days, afraid this was all a big mistake.

I read *Newsweek* and *National Geographic* cover to cover before the bus arrived. Finally, the loudspeaker announced his arrival and I stood up from the plastic waiting-room chair, stiff and nervous. I searched the tinted windows of the Greyhound for the face of my son and realized I would know him only by his resemblance to the pictures Susan sent each year at Christmas. I could see nothing except shadows moving forward, jostling to pull luggage from overhead racks—gray shapes coming one by one, blinking as they stepped into the light.

And there he was—Jonas, still two and a half in my mind, appearing suddenly in the doorway as an eight-year-old. He was his mother's child—dark, tall for his age, thin and wiry like I never was and never likely will be.

I waved as he stepped to the pavement. He glanced at me, then looked away, his face expressionless.

"Jonas," I said, and his name sounded strange said out loud. I extended my hand to shake his and I was suddenly aware of how it might feel to him—fleshy, damp with all the waiting, a hand to let go of quickly.

"I thought you'd be smaller," he said, and it caught me off guard. Was he being mean, had he inherited his mother's knack for condescension? But he was smiling and I noticed he had a bottom tooth missing, which was reassuring, and then I realized that any pictures he'd seen of me were old ones and though I had watched him grow in snapshots over the last five years, he had no such gauge for my own expansion in another direction. Anyway, how nice of him to substitute the word "smaller" for "thinner."

"Whatever picture you saw was at least five years of fudge sundaes ago."

He laughed. What a relief!

The first thing he did was pull a folded Muni map from a canvas shoulder bag. He unfolded it carefully and asked me, "So where's the hotel?"

"Post Street, near Taylor."

He ran his finger down a crowded column of numbers until he came to one highlighted by a yellow marker.

"We can take the number 27 Bryant," he said, "then walk a couple of blocks."

"You're a good person to travel with, I can see that," I said.

For weeks I'd been trying to anticipate a boy nervous about seeing his father for the first time since he was nearly three, arriving in a strange city to meet a stranger. At work I gave out wrong numbers, I talked to people too long—things a directory assistance operator is trained against doing. I was reprimanded by my supervisor. I was warned to pay more attention.

"How about taking a cab—it'll be faster." There. An offering of speed, assurance.

He looked at me, raising his eyes from the map to meet mine. He sighed, looking for a way to be patient. I'd missed the point.

"But I want to take the bus. I *came here* to take the bus. And I know how to get there."

I wasn't about to start off trying to change his mind. And I had come, in a way, to put myself in his hands. Besides, I couldn't remember the last time I was on a bus—I always rode my bicycle to work. "OK, you win," I said, grinning at him, but he was still serious, studying the map.

"We'll need exact change. Ninety cents altogether."

I dug in my pocket and pulled out a paltry offering of coins—two dimes, three pennies, and a nickel.

Jonas took a zippered coin purse out of his canvas bag. It was divided into small compartments. Jonas had filed his coins away, separated the denominations. He fished three quarters from the largest compartment.

"I've got it," he said, then took the dime and nickel from my still open hand.

I looked at my son as he held our now exact combined change and did a perfect refolding job on the map. He didn't get any of this from me, or Susan either. I remembered Gibran: "Children are not from you, they are passing through you." It made sense. Jonas *was* passing through, as if he'd already sensed my own aimless confusion across the years, rejected that legacy, and found a means to know exactly where he was going and how to get there.

A white bus with a red and orange logo, the word "Muni" barely legible, pulled into the stop, its brakes shrieking. When Jonas stepped up in front of the till he funneled our fare into it, then said to the driver, "Transfer." He held up two fingers, then pointed to me. "Can you call out at Post?" The driver, a black man in a beret and dark aviator glasses, looked at me. Maybe he thought I was blind or retarded, that Jonas was leading me around. I wanted to defend myself though I'd been accused of nothing.

"Sure thing," he said to Jonas. "Right after Geary."

Jonas thanked him. I could almost imagine the two of them having a lengthy, animated conversation, discussing routes, transfer points, fare hikes. Excluding me.

"Step to the rear of the coach," the driver said, looking into his rearview mirror at the jumble of people and shopping bags piled up like a logjam in the front of the bus. Jonas nodded when the driver repeated the phrase with the same inflection and cadence as before, like a recording.

"They have to say that—people don't ever think of it themselves," Jonas said to me.

"Sheep," I agreed.

"Baa-aa." Jonas giggled, then stood there bleating some more. Someone laughed, and echoed him. I was surprised—it seemed like such a kid thing to do and already I'd started thinking of him as an adult in an undersized body.

We made our way to the rear of the bus and found a place to sit just in front of the last seat. A man in a turban and sunglasses, dressed, of all things, in a plaid kilt and red Converse high-tops, held a transistor radio six inches from his ear. It was incredibly loud, but he probably couldn't hear it through the turban. He was listening to a religious talk show where people called up and argued about Jesus' nationality and actual hair color. Nobody, but nobody, met that man's gaze.

Jonas turned around, pointed to the hand-lettered regulations on the curved wall above the windows and read the words for him.

"Radios must be silenced."

The man with the radio stared at Jonas as if he'd said an incomprehensible thing.

"I can read," he said, rather petulantly.

"Turn it off then. Please," Jonas said, not in a mean or challenging way, just that modulated tone the driver used to get us moving to the rear. But I stared straight ahead, terrified, wishing we had stayed in front instead of venturing into the nether regions at the back of the bus.

The noise stopped abruptly.

When the driver called out "Post," the word sailed toward us and I felt a kind of thrill as Jonas rang the bell in answer.

❖ In the hotel room I got out my guidebooks while Jonas spread his BART and Muni route maps on both beds. He stood between them, referring to one, then the other. He obviously wasn't the kind of kid that had to be constantly entertained. The entire two-day weekend would be filled with route numbers, inbound and outbound schedules. I picked out destinations from my book and then he went to work, figuring out how to get us there.

He ordered room service for us both—a grilled cheese and orange juice for him, cheeseburger and sundae for me. I didn't ask for the sundae and was surprised when I heard him say it into the phone. "No maraschino cherry," he said to whoever listened on the other end.

"How do you know about room service?" I asked.

"Mom took me to Las Vegas once, on one of her business trips. I had to pretty much stay in the room while she went to meetings, so I just ordered whatever I wanted while she was gone."

I pictured him on the thirty-ninth floor of some high-rise hotel, surrounded by trays, waiting all day for Susan to come back with her briefcase full of software manuals. The thought of it made me heartsick.

We ate our lunch and plotted our route to Fisherman's Wharf. It seemed a logical first place to go. I suggested Alcatraz, too.

"Where's that?"

"It's an island—in the bay."

"Then there's no bus?"

"No—you take a ferry."

He shook his head. "Then I don't want to go."

I laughed. "OK. Fine. We can go to Ghirardelli Square instead—it's a chocolate factory. I'm sure the bus stops there."

Jonas pored over his maps, his dark brows set in a line of deep concentration as he figured the city out. He carefully refolded his maps and put them into the pockets of his canvas bag. We set the room service trays outside the door and walked to the elevator.

"Want to push the button?" I asked, thinking he, like all kids, would like to press the whole row of orange heat-sensitive squares before you can stop them.

"No thanks," Jonas said. "You go ahead." He wasn't interested in vertical travel at all.

I'd been so worried that the divorce would have made him a sad, private child full of fears and insecurities. But there we were, trudging up Post Street. I couldn't stop stealing glances at our reflection in the gallery windows.

We headed for Polk Street to catch the bus to Ghirardelli. The number 19, Jonas told me. We passed a bus stop shelter on a corner where there was no one waiting and when a bus stopped in front of it to let a woman off, Jonas pulled a hard left and let go of my hand as he climbed on the bus. I stood on the curb, unsure of what to do.

"Come *on*," he said, turning from the top step to look back at me.

"What number is this?" I asked, afraid he'd made a mistake. It seemed to me that bus was going in the wrong direction.

"I don't know." He looked annoyed with my hesitancy.

"Well why did you get on if you don't know—I thought you always know where you're going."

"I want to take this one."

"Let's go," the driver said dully. "On or off, what'll it be?"

I got on. Jonas settled into a seat and waited for me to take the seat next to him. So I sat.

The bus was nearly empty and rolled down the steep hills of the city, its till rattling, coins shivering when we hit the potholes. Soon we were out of the shadows of tall downtown buildings, into the brighter space of low warehouses, wider streets, fewer people. The smell of salt water drifted through the doors when they opened.

The bus slowed to a stop to pick up a man with a seeing-eye dog.

"Let's get off here," Jonas said.

The dog waited for us to get off, trained for a patience that would not be natural to an animal at all, then it slowly led the man up the steps, pausing after each one for the man to get his bearings.

The bus left us standing on the sidewalk. I looked around. There was nothing there but warehouses.

"Why did we get off here?"

"It looked nice."

I looked around again, but I couldn't for the life of me see what he thought was worth getting off for. A row of brick warehouses. Papers rustling in the windy street.

"Up there," he said, pointing to a row of windows just catching the late afternoon sun. In a few minutes they would be dull gray with dusk, but he had looked up at the precise moment when they were gilded with light. We stood there with our necks craned, as if the windows' luminescence flashed a message only Jonas could see, that I could see too if I looked long enough. We were pulled upward by bright windows, by more than reflected light on glass, as if something extraordinary pulsed in the rooms behind them.

❖ It was dark by the time the 42 Sansome picked us up. Jonas seemed tired and leaned against me in the seat. As we stopped at a traffic light, Jonas sat up and pointed across the street to a brightly lit deli on the corner.

"Let's eat there," he said.

"I thought we were going to the wharf—I know a place where they have great seafood."

"But we're here," he said emphatically, as if the exact moment of his hunger had been answered by the appearance of a place to satiate it. He stood up and pulled the bell and the back doors opened as he stood on the treadle step. The doors closed again and the bus sailed on without us.

We both ordered cheese blintzes and sat at a formica table beneath humming fluorescent tubes. The orange plastic booths glared. It wasn't a place that made you want to linger, but Jonas seemed oblivious to the decor and concentrated on icing his blintzes with jam and sour cream.

"How did you get to like buses so much?"

He looked up, leveled his eyes at me as if trying to determine why I asked him this. He shrugged.

"Our next-door neighbor—Mr. Sykes—is a bus driver. He takes me on his route in the afternoons and drops me off at Mom's office when she gets off work. His bus goes right by there."

"Where else does the bus go?"

"Out to the end of the line. Salt Aire Beach. We wait ten minutes, then go back the way we came." He scooped another bite of blintz dripping with cream into his mouth, dropped some on his T-shirt.

I pictured my son and Mr. Sykes sitting at the end of the line, staring out the windows at the briny waters of the great Salt Lake, the Wasatch Front rearing blue in the evening behind them. Mr. Sykes would let him push the button that sent the doors whooshing open and closed. I could see the bus sitting there in the sandy turnaround. The doors opened and closed, opened and closed.

"What about trains or cable cars—do you like to ride them too?"

"Not as much. They can only go on tracks. If a car breaks down on the tracks in front of them they can't go around. They have to just sit and wait." He takes another bite, then says emphatically, "And wait and wait and wait."

I tried to imagine him sitting on a streetcar immobilized like a ship run aground, the driver out of his seat, out on the street talking with other drivers in the luxurious span of unexpected free time while Jonas fidgeted in his seat, crushing his transfer to the consistency of Kleenex in the close heat of his small hand. And I could almost picture him checking his watch if Mr. Sykes didn't pick him up on time. I was glad that I made it to the bus terminal in time to meet him. And then it struck me that there were at least a hundred other simple ways that I could let him down, and probably would, without meaning to. So much could go wrong in such a short time. One slip and he might write me off forever. I might be his father, but Mr. Sykes knew him better than I did, had given him something he could count on as surely as anything in this world—an origin, a destination, a clearly defined route, an end-of-the-line satisfaction that always meant beginning again.

❖ Jonas got us back to the hotel. As we stepped into the elevator and I pushed our floor number, he leaned back, satisfied. He had ventured out into a strange city and already mapped a part of it in his brain, gone out into the void and found his way back again.

Jonas brushed his teeth, folded his clothes, and put them in a bureau drawer.

"Good-night, Dad," he called in a sleepy, husky voice from the bed, so different from the wide-awake voice I'd always heard on the telephone when I called every year on his birthday. He'd called me Dad on the phone, but hearing it in the same room was different, like listening to an anthem played right in front of you instead of through the stereo or the TV. I could have kissed him for that, but didn't know if he would let me.

"Good-night, Jonas. See you in the morning."

He fell asleep immediately. I heard his breathing slow and deepen. I turned out the reading lamp and in the faint light that seeped around the paper window shade from the streetlamp just outside the window I made my way to his bed. It floated like a raft in the semi-darkness. I sat on the edge. My hand hovered in the air above his dark head on the white pillow. And then his body jerked in spasm and he made a moaning kind of sound, though his mouth didn't open. His eyebrows arched, then furrowed, then arched again, though they stayed closed. He was flailing, netted and caught in the dry sheets of his bed. And then he was still again.

A siren echoed far off, then came closer, and as the red lights raced along the wall, my hand floated again, without hesitation, and came down softly, shielding his ear against the shrill and hopeless cry of someone else's emergency.

❖ When I opened my eyes Jonas was sitting on the edge of the bed in his pajamas, the room service menu balanced on his knees and the phone cradled between his shoulder and his ear.

"Orange juice. Two French toasts. Extra butter," he said.

"Coffee," I mumbled.

He turned toward the sound. "Coffee," he repeated. "Cream," he said, remembering how I drank it last night.

I couldn't remember ever feeling so taken care of.

Over breakfast we made some plans. Fisherman's Wharf. China-town. Golden Gate Park. Jonas studied his maps.

"Number 15 Third, 19 Polk, 38 Geary."

I called Scoma's and made a reservation at noon for lunch, then we headed out into the thick morning fog, bundled up even though it was July. We took the number 15 Third to Chinatown and walked up Grant Avenue from Clay.

Jonas stood gaping in front of a window of coppery barbequed ducks that hung upside down, their bills sealed with glaze. Strange vegetables formed tiers that rose from wooden crates. I named them for him, "Bok choy, lemongrass, lychee nuts," like a father pointing out different trees on a forest walk. He nodded, excited, and I felt flushed with joy.

He picked up a blue Chairman Mao cap at a table outside a shop.

"Go ahead—try it on."

He did and he looked great, really great in it. So I got it for him, and as we walked down the street I kept looking at his reflection in store windows and each time I was surprised at the resemblance that formed, more evident diffused in glass than looking straight on. I thought I was starting to look more like him all the time.

❖ We picked up the 15 Third again at Broadway. "Hello again," the driver said. We'd stayed long enough in Chinatown for him to make a complete circle and come back to us. Jonas was pleased, I could tell, and smiled like someone who expected synchronicity from life instead of being astounded by it.

As we settled in our seat I took a look at my watch. Eleven-thirty. We'd make it just in time for lunch.

We passed a green city block, a park lined with walkways and trees, and two old men near a jungle gym, poised and motionless in a tai chi stance. Jonas reached up and yanked on the bell twice.

"What are you doing?"

"I want to get off," he said, annoyed, as if I'd asked the stupid kind of question only adults can come up with, a question he'd already explained.

My own annoyance rose, full-blown, to the challenge. "We're supposed to be at Scoma's at noon." I pointed at the hand on my watch for emphasis, for empirical effect.

Before I could say another thing Jonas was out the door and I had to bolt from my seat to keep from losing him altogether.

I stepped to the curb and there he was, giving me that steady neutral gaze again, his eyes shadowed by the visor of the cap, but his body was half turned away as if expecting to be chased.

"I thought we were going to the wharf for lunch. You said you wanted to go," and as soon as I said it I heard the absurd whine in my voice.

"But this is better," he said, looking over his shoulder, pointing at the two black-clad men, their bodies pointing, graceful as herons lifting their long legs in shallow water.

I was torn between standing my ground and bending as I watched the men slowly turn, both supple and brittle in their bones. Hadn't I spent the sixties trying to untie myself from rules and regulations, and hadn't I failed at that too? We all thought that, as the Bible said, a child would be the one to lead us. But where was he going? And did I really want to go along?

"Look," I told him. "You're not the only one on this vacation. I'm not just along for the ride—I want to go to the wharf like we planned."

He looked up at me, surprised, but didn't argue. I went on.

"And don't do that again—don't just jump up like that and bolt out the door. It scares me." I was waving my arms in the air and suddenly felt ridiculous, wildly gesticulating so close to the graceful movements of the old men.

Jonas ignored me, turned to watch the men who seemed as if they would lift themselves from the ground and take flight.

I stared at his turned-away face until I realized that he was making a place for me to speak and that if I didn't open my mouth soon it would be too late. All my life I had let other people—my father, Susan, my boss, my landlord, even creditors on the telephone—say things to me that left me speechless, shriveled and flattened by wills stronger than my own.

"Jonas, please look at me."

"What for?"

My hands were shaking, my voice rose louder than I'd intended.

"When you ignore me like that it's like being invisible. I *hate* the way that feels."

He turned back slowly. He looked lost, the way a celestial navigator would look if the North Star had just fallen from the sky.

"Jonas, I want to get back on a bus to the wharf and I want you to come with me."

He looked almost relieved that I had a plan.

"So let's go," he said.

❖ By the time we made it to Scoma's we were late and the bar was filled with business people with long lunch hours. Neither of us wanted to wait.

We walked down the block and I bought two overpriced crab cocktails in dixie cups, then we wandered back toward Scoma's, to the dock behind the restaurant. We leaned against the railing and looked out over the boats in the marina, a thicket of masts jutting from their hulls like so many pins stuck in a pincushion. Behind us at least a dozen cats sat patiently near the back door of Scoma's waiting for the heads and fins to fly their way. Jonas had his eyes on the cats; I turned toward the water and spread the map out on the railing.

Jonas put his paper cup down. Several cats made a beeline for it, sniffed, discerning the odor of shrimp lost beneath the acrid tomato sauce. They veered away without a single tentative lick and took up their stations by the door again.

"Now what do we do?" he said.

I hesitated for a few seconds. My normal tactic would be to defer, to shrug and make someone else decide, something that had always driven Susan crazy. What the hell, I thought, all he can do is disagree.

"I'd like to go to the beach. Come with?"

He nodded. This was easier than I thought.

"You drive," I said, handing him the map.

❖ We took the 19 Polk, transferred at Market to the L Taraval trolley (he liked the name). It was a green and yellow streetcar that hummed with electrical power, rocking from the shifting weight of passengers getting on and off.

"I thought you didn't like things that drove on tracks."

"Mr. Sykes used to drive a trolley before they tore up the tracks. I wanted to see what they're like."

The trolley plunged into a tunnel. The lights came on and we flew through the dark, unimpeded by traffic signals, intersections. We flew flat out into the heart of the mountain. Then suddenly we broke out into the light of a different world as if the mountain held back the city and its narrow, shadowed streets. On the other side, it was all low houses and a long glide down to the metallic flare of the sea, gray beneath a foggy sky.

I watched the street signs pass, the gradually ascending numbers. Jonas sat calmly, his hands folded across the map. It was the longest we'd gone in one direction.

"Are you sure this goes to the beach?" I asked.

"It goes close—to the turnaround at the end of the line."

We left the business district behind at Twenty-fifth Avenue. The wide avenues held endless, orderly rows of stucco houses and sample-sized lawns, people with hoses out suckling their shrubs.

At Forty-eighth the trolley went off to a siding and stopped. The electricity faltered, then the humming disappeared. Neither of us moved or said a thing. Now what? I thought to myself. I watched the driver because I couldn't think of anything else to do right then. He opened the door and went across the street to a corner grocery.

He came out in a minute with a Styrofoam cup of coffee and leaned against the building, one leg up like a stork, his sole pressed flat against the graffiti-covered wall. He lit a cigarette and sipped the coffee that added its steam to the fog in the air.

I could hear the waves, but I couldn't see them. A low hill blocked the view, but I saw a pedestrian subway, and at the end of that short tunnel the gray ocean narrowed to a telescope view.

Jonas didn't move from his seat.

"Don't you want to see the ocean?" I asked.

"No, I just want to listen to it."

"But I want to see it. They don't have one in Montana."

He followed me reluctantly through the pedestrian underpass and our footsteps sounded huge until the concrete sidewalk disappeared at the end of the tunnel and we trudged through sand.

I fully expected him to go charging off once he saw the water, to run right up to the surf like he did when he was two, but he stayed close by and seemed to draw back inside himself the closer we got to shore.

The fog hung low over the water, and the setting sun turned pewter behind the clouds. A gull whirled above us and we tilted our heads back to watch. A wave caught us then, sloshed over our sneakers with frothy suds, and we shrieked and jumped as it soaked into our socks.

"These are my only shoes!" Jonas cried.

"They'll dry."

"No, they won't," he wailed.

"So we'll take them off."

He sat down with an expression that said he had no intention of budging. He watched me, shocked, as I pulled my own sneakers off, then reached to unknot the laces of his.

"They're double knots," he said belligerently and folded his arms across his chest, bringing the knots to three.

It took a while—the wet laces seemed glued together and my fingers felt stupidly thick, all the dexterity leached out of them—

but finally the laces pulled free. I pulled the shoes off carefully, peeled the socks down slowly. His feet looked so small, so white and unprotected. So untried and tender.

I rolled up my pants and waded into the surf. I saw something move beyond the breakwater.

"Look, Jonas, a sea lion!"

"Where?" His voice was hard, ungiving.

I looked back at him. He looked miserable sitting there hugging himself, squinting hard at the water.

"There." I pointed at the breakwater, where a sleek, dark head bobbed just above the rolling waves.

I turned back toward him and held out my hand.

"Come on. You'll miss it."

He stood up, stepped warily into the water, prancing at the cold shock of it on his toes. A wave came in fast and he lunged forward to grab my hand as the water crashed around my shins, his knees.

The sea lion barked twice and slipped beneath the water. When it surfaced again it was closer, its black eyes gazing at us, huge and curious.

"It sees us!" Jonas cried.

I tried to see us too from the perspective of a sea lion rising effortlessly on the swells, a new portrait painted over the older, darker work where a man searched for his son in the churning water. In the new one, the sea was brighter and we were two land creatures joined at the hands, one dark and thin, the other blond and round, knee deep in water as gray-green as our eyes. In this picture we were waving, as if someone had just called out to us and we answered because we heard and thought we knew them.

❖ *News from Another World*

I've been in this nursing home nine years now and I've seen more than a few strange things, but it's the babies that can make a person do a thing they wouldn't dream of doing otherwise. The last time they brought the babies, I stayed in my room and locked the door and it took three nurses to talk me into coming out again. The people from the orphanage who brought them were surprised—I suppose they thought the babies would cheer us up. Nobody here would admit it, but we get used to the routine and fiercely protect it from the outside, wary as immigrants in a new country.

They're bringing them back this morning. They figure two weeks is enough time for us to settle down again. They usually bring them in the morning when we're most awake and generally in a good mood. Mornings always make me feel hopeful. They're as clear of disappointments and failures as the Monday morning blackboards at the Greenpoint Primary school, where I spent forty-five years teaching. I always liked them when I walked in—the janitor had washed them over the weekend, and the smooth black surface seemed like it would

make the first thing written on it in white chalk look like the abso-
lute truth before the eraser turned it muddy with the ghosts of old
equations showing through.

❖ When the babies have been carried into the dayroom, Mrs. Valenzuela greets us all in a loud voice. I'm sitting by the picture window,
the one with the bird feeder dangling from the eaves on the other
side of the glass. Beyond the trees, Manhattan looms in the distance,
but the haze is usually so thick you can't make it out. On clear days
it surprises you, the way it's been there all along, as definite as a
mountain.

I'm wearing a yellow knit cardigan today and choose the window
seat to be near the birds. I read that babies like loud colors and moving things and if I decide to hold one today, which I probably won't,
I want to be able to interest it enough to keep it from crying.

I'll pretend to read a magazine. If they catch on that you like something they can use it against you later—a bargaining tool to blud-
geon you with: "If you don't take your medication, then you won't
get to watch the video on Saturday. Now wouldn't that be a shame?"
Then they answer for you. "Well, yes, it certainly would. Now take
your pill like a good girl." Girl. I always pretend to take my pill like
the crafty old woman I've become. I tuck it in my cheek and pretend
to swallow till the nurse has gone, then stick it in the hem of my robe.
I don't like the sluggish feeling these pills give me. I'd rather lose
sleep, sit up and watch the shadows of the trees, the headlights along
Flatbush Avenue. It's the only peaceful time here. I can turn my memories over slowly like black cards coming down over the red, sequen-
tial, ordered; and like I cheat in solitaire, I can reshuffle until I come
up with the ace.

If Vera were alive she'd say, "One baby's not enough—give me
two to hold!" She was brash for someone who was completely blind.
I spent fifteen years across the hall from Vera in our apartment building on Greenpoint Avenue. People were drawn to her like I was for
the ease of her company, her unpredictable laughter. We could walk

into the door of her one-room apartment, slouch in her comfortable chairs, unpin our hair or loosen our ties. We forgot our strictness with ourselves around Vera as if we too could enter an unbounded darkness and find there a tolerance, a kinder look at ourselves.

"Mrs. Hulfish!" Mrs. Valenzuela calls out my name incorrectly, too brightly for my taste, and I wince into my *Time* magazine.

"*Miss* Hulfish," I say with appropriate indignation. But she goes on.

"Would you like to hold Luis today?"

I shrug and don't put the magazine down right away. Let her work a little harder. Truth is, if I liked babies, which I don't especially, I would like Luis. He's sturdy—the kind of baby you could take on a train and he wouldn't be scared by the noise, wouldn't be sick when the world flashed by the window.

Mr. Henderson has already got his. Lucinda with the tiny gold earrings in her lobes bounces happily on his rickety knee. Like Vera, Mr. Henderson is always the first to join in whatever new they've got going on here. He just rushes right out and grabs on to life as if it's still willing to greet him, still got something good in store.

I flip one more page and make like I'm reading intently, but it's only an ad for a car perched precariously on some national landmark in Arizona, so I fold it up and put it down and feel immediately unprotected. I look at my watch first as if I might have an appointment somewhere, then I look at Mrs. Valenzuela.

"Don't you want to hold him?" she says.

"I'm too old."

"Nonsense!" Mrs. Valenzuela raises her eyebrows—two crescents as thin as fingernails rising into the furrows of her forehead.

"Too old," I repeat. They've been trying to get me to take a baby now for weeks and I've finally thought of a good reason why I won't.

"Are you afraid you'll drop him? The nurse tells me you've healed from your injury, that you're strong enough now."

I look out the window. Why I don't want that baby on my lap is that he might know my fear the way horses do when you ride them badly, that he might cry and I wouldn't be able to stop it—tears have a way of getting completely out of hand if you let them start. And then I couldn't think of him as a possibility anymore. I would have used up my turn and he would forever associate me with something he didn't like. People hold grudges, I know. There's nothing about me left that would be soothing to a child.

But I've said the wrong thing. Mrs. Valenzuela is taking this as a personal challenge, and Luis's abundant bottom is brought down to my bony lap.

"There," she says, as if his very weight proved her theory. "He likes you, see?"

But Luis is transfixed by the flurry of wings at the feeder and I am just something he leans against to get a better view. So I watch the birds with him for a while, and if I hold him wrong or jiggle him too much he doesn't let on. The birds are everything to him, enough to hold all of his attention and then some, and I think how lovely it must be to be so completely distracted by something that it doesn't matter who's holding you or who isn't, that it doesn't matter where you are or where you aren't that you'd rather be.

❖ When the babies leave, the dayroom's noise subsides—all that laughter and crying. The noise of extremes folds into itself again, leaving us to our own familiar drone—the slapping of cards on the formica table, the constant clearing of Mr. Milo's throat, Hattie Turnbull playing "Moon River" on the upright piano, pedal to the floor like she's driving somewhere fast. The TV blares. The intercom crackles with the voice of one nurse calling another. There's no such thing as peace and quiet. Like the babies, we've all learned to sleep through cacophony.

I go out into the garden and sit on the wrought-iron bench but there's a mockingbird in the branch of a dead tree filling up the air with one song after another. Every so often it flies at the window attacking its own reflection.

The mockingbird's singlemindedness shows no signs of letting up. I leave him to his hopeless task of evoking response from his hard reflection and rise slowly from the bench, unbending myself by degrees. My sciatic nerve burns red-hot in the muscle as I shuffle down the path to put in my quarter mile before dinner. I long for that point in this daily routine where I forget myself for half an hour in the brief triumph of my second wind, where my body works of its own accord, tendons expand and contract in the rhythm of an easy stride. There's an aluminum can that has rolled onto the path. I take aim and kick it into the bushes. And then I feel myself go over, slowly, like a bicycle pushed off its kickstand by the wind. The grass they never get around to mowing here looks as thick as a rain forest so close to my face. I could probably move but I don't feel like it right now. If I've hurt myself again I don't want to know it yet. I just want to lie here in this brief grace, face up to the sky.

The clouds move at dizzying speed, last leaves rattle on their stems. I can't stop it. I swirl with sickening speed toward a memory. I'm lying in a field in Vermont. The breeze brings the strong dark scent of burning leaves from the house below the field. My belly rises, my body a hill blending with the hill that arches beneath my back. In the house below, eight women in various stages of gestation move among the rooms, waiting to return to the acceptable shapes of single girls. Farthest along, I will be the first to leave. We are all making up the stories of our long, unexpected vacations, imagining what souvenirs could be used as alibis, what postcards would be most convincing— this lake, that mountain where we rested for a while.

The ground is damp now and my dress feels cold against my skin. I roll myself over and grab onto the skinny trunk of a newly planted tree and hoist myself back into the vertical world. My feet and hands work fine—nothing broken or sprained, no damage done— but I am stiff, and when I begin to walk I feel as cumbersome as an astronaut back on earth who still remembers the weightless feel of space.

I walk into the dining hall where everyone has just sat down to dinner. Heads turn toward me. Emma Pinski, looking a bit glazed, says, "Althea, where on earth have you been? They've been looking for you." Her tone is accusing because I've disrupted a sure thing—Saturday, chicken "à la King" and carrot purée. And then in the mirror along the wall I see what they see—leaves stuck in my hair which has escaped from the clench of its pins and combs, a torn stocking letting my bony knee protrude, a green smear of grass across my sleeve. I have returned like a traveler from an unplanned adventure and I feel the slow, hidden smile of a bad girl begin.

❖ Before breakfast, an ambulance comes for Mr. Henderson. He walks in his sleep and this time the police picked him up at a corner grocery down on Flatbush. He was standing talking into a pay phone in his bathrobe and slippers for an hour before the clerk came out to check on him. There was no one on the other end of the line.

They're taking him to St. Joe's this morning for treatment of some kind. What I remember about hospitals is how the mask comes down over your face and darkness seeps behind your eyes and while you're under they take something from you—pull it right out of your body. Afterward, there's the emptiness on the other side of anesthesia, the feeling of flatness where something round was before.

The mood is subdued in the dayroom. No "Moon River" this morning. Mrs. Flannery, tied to her electric wheelchair, has fallen asleep with her hand on the lever, and the chair whirls slowly in a small circle like something caught in the centrifugal force around a drain.

Mr. Henderson comes back in the late afternoon, his head bobbing like a heavy flower on the thin stalk of his neck. I walk five times around the path, twice my usual amount, but I can't get to my second wind, can't get Henderson's face out of my mind. I'm on the sixth lap when they rap on the window to summon me to dinner.

❖ I can't sleep. Tomorrow is Thanksgiving and the day after that the babies are coming. So I'm up past midnight, feeling for my slippers under the bed. My hand touches the radiator—cold. Not so much as a whisper through the pipes. I find my flannel robe on its hook inside the closet and slip out the door. I head toward the dayroom. By night it's as empty and dark as a stage after the audience has gone home. I smell the cigarette smoke before I see the orange glow of the lit end moving near the window. Henderson sits in a big wing chair that folds around him, and his knees are splayed out in resignation. I think about sitting with him but I'm not sure if he's doing this in his sleep or, if he's awake, if he would even remember me.

❖ Holidays. Relatives who still come to visit invariably come on these obligatory days and their visits draw a line between The Claimed and the rest of us, The Unvisited Ones. My sister Harriet came, for a few weeks anyway, after she signed me into this place. Before I got here, Harriet would call when she was too sad to speak straight or needed a loan—back when I still had money that belonged to me—but when I broke my hip the day after Vera's funeral by falling down the stairs in my apartment building, Harriet started making decisions for me. The accident was the perfect proof that Harriet had been looking for to shame me with. "You need to be somewhere you'll be taken care of," she said, which was another way of saying "You can't stay with me." She was scared to death of me needing anything from her.

The bones weren't going back together right and during that healing time that took longer than anybody expected I lost more than my ability to walk. I lost the confidence I used to have in my body—I was a strong swimmer in my day from regular practice at the Y—and in that helplessness which I gave in to as if it were ether pulling me away from the world, I lost the right to take care of myself. I had the unwanted distinction of having outlived the few friends I'd had. I resigned myself to coming here but didn't go out of my way to be friendly. What's the point? I thought. People in the same boat are never there because they want to be. We just grow accustomed to one another, joined in the tedious habits of survival, the same way Mrs. McCarthy talks about her walker—said it was a strange thing at first, a hindrance, and a downright embarrassment. After a while she got sort of grafted onto it and now she leans into it, half kneeling like it's a metal pew that will invariably support her, a private church she takes with her everywhere.

By noon on Thanksgiving day, those with visitors are steered out the double swinging doors past the forever misspelled sign that says "The Tender Loveing Care Home for the Elderly" into waiting cars idling in the drive, their interiors flushed with steady heat, their windows steamed with the breath of children.

At four o'clock those of us remaining come into the dining room, drifting uncertainly to the single table that floats like an island in the center of the enormous room. The table is skirted with a long flounce of orange crepe paper that rustles every time one of us shifts our weight or recrosses our legs. Cardboard turkeys lean against our water glasses and fall flat as if shot from behind any time one of us takes a drink.

Mr. Henderson comes through the doorway just as the purée-of-pumpkin soup is served.

"Ship of Fools—becalmed," he says crossing the waveless surface of the wooden floor. "The S.S. *Tender Loveing Care* has sailed out of radar range. No one knows where we are."

Everyone studies their soup, nervous that he is on the loose and might do something more unpredictable awake than asleep. But I am so very relieved to see him acting his old self again that I laugh and Henderson gives me a jaunty salute which I almost return.

Emma Pinski sits next to me, swaying slightly with sedatives. She aims the serving spoon into the cranberry sauce which is still in the shape of the can it came from, the circles of the can perfectly imprinted on the murky crimson jell.

"Food of the gods," Henderson says with a smirk.

Mr. Penner, with his perpetual expression of withering scorn, carefully puts down his turkey wing in the small clearing on his plate. "Now there's no need to be sarcastic. I, for one, am trying to enjoy my meal."

"There is every need to be sarcastic, especially here," Henderson says, banging the thick handle of his butter knife on the table. "It keeps me from falling asleep at the wheel."

"But you don't have a car," Emma cries, fixing on the word "wheel" as a sound she recognizes that is connected to an image she can still clearly recall.

"Precisely." Henderson smiles.

I'm enjoying this. I put my elbows squarely on the table and lean into them and Henderson, directly opposite me, leans too and then I feel the unmistakable pressure of his knee meeting mine.

But Mr. Penner is getting more agitated by the minute. He picks up the wing again and wrestles with it, trying to unfold the bones to get at the meat. "It's precisely because you *do* fall asleep at the wheel that you were taken out of here yesterday. You probably don't remember how to drive anymore." The wing snaps and he bites savagely into the meat which I am happy to see still has several unplucked hairs bristling from the skin.

Henderson stands up so quickly his chair goes over backward and crashes to the floor. Penner brandishes the bone. "You better settle down, or they'll tie you to your bed!"

Henderson marches over to the upright piano by the far wall.

"Why don't you stop being so difficult?" I shout at Penner, surprised by the volume my voice is suddenly capable of after the long silence I've kept here. And I don't want to stop now—I've got some momentum going. "You are behaving like a perfect bastard." I'm surprised, too, at the swear word that seventy years' memory of the taste of soap has kept down for so long. It was as if Vera leaned close for a minute and whispered it in my ear.

Henderson pushes the piano away from the wall with some difficulty and I rush to help him although I haven't the faintest idea where he wants to go with it or what he'll do when he gets there. It's a heavy thing and its tiny wheels shriek with disuse. We're heading toward the kitchen, Henderson steering the thing as best he can, and before I know it we've barricaded the doors.

"No dessert for you!" Henderson shouts back at Penner.

He bends over the keys and pounds out a thundering rendition of "Dixie." None of us knew he could play or that the South might be a place he missed, and it strikes me how little any of us knows about anyone else here except our present quirks and idiosyncrasies.

Two faces appear like framed photographs in the small windows in the swinging doors. The doors won't budge an inch. Pounding comes from the other side.

For about thirty seconds I feel victorious. The music soars and echoes in the room for a time. And then out of the corner of my eye, I see a blur of white come through the undefended doors on the other side of the room and I hear Penner's indignant cry as we're led away. "I'm not moving until I get my *pie.*" And Henderson's brief struggle, an orderly at either side, the glint of the needle going in.

Dark comes early and we are all sent to bed. Tonight I don't put the sedative in the hem of my robe. Tonight I want the blankness of enforced sleep. Tonight I've seen enough.

❖ Henderson isn't at breakfast, and Emma says when she passed by his room he wasn't there and his bed was made. Either they've taken him away or he's driving in his sleep on Flatbush Avenue again. No one seems to know for sure, so I imagine him the way I want to, behind the wheel of an old, heavy car, driving at an elegant, sedate speed, Tommy Dorsey on the radio, the smoke of a Lucky Strike curling out the open window.

❖ The babies come in the afternoon. Mrs. Valenzuela seems surprised when I walk right up to her and ask for Luis but she's smart enough not to make a fuss about it.

I want Luis to myself for a while. I drift into the garden, away from the noise, and take him to the bench near the place where I fell and prop him up there next to me, my arm around him to keep him from tipping over.

There's a cool breeze that thins the warmth of the sun this close to December. On such a day as this I went into labor and was taken to the county hospital where they left the father's name blank next to mine on the certificate. I had such bad pains they put me under.

When I woke I was in the maternity ward, emptied, my heart pounding with the last of the ether. They wouldn't tell me if it was a girl or a boy. They referred to it as "the baby" and said it would soon be in the hands of a couple that were better suited to take care of it. It didn't seem right that it was taken that way, that I couldn't give it away myself. I never felt so alone in all my life, before or since, except the time when I fell down my back stairs before anyone found me— both times I was reminded how incapable I was of taking care of things. Two nights of loving in a field with a boy I'd known all my life had produced a child that was mine only as long as it was hidden inside me. The moment it was brought to light it was gone. After a while I couldn't even imagine it anymore.

I went home to my parents in Staten Island who never treated me like someone they wanted to trust again. I finished high school at home and then I went to a teacher's college in Brooklyn. For forty-five years I had a predictable, ordered life. I had my friends, but I led, at least in the eyes of the world, a solitary life because I never let a man that close to me again.

❖ An ambulance pulls up to the back entrance and I hoist Luis onto my good hip and make my way there. The ambulance attendants open the doors of the van and roll a gurney down the ramp. Henderson lies strapped to it like a corpse on a board about to be slipped over the side into the deep. His eyes are open. I take his hand.

"You a relation?" the driver says to me.

I look at Henderson, then at Luis. "Yes. I've brought our grandchild for a visit." To Henderson I say, "Where on earth have you been?"

The ambulance driver answers for him. "Out at Far Rockaway, taking a stroll on the boardwalk, sound asleep."

I look at Henderson and his eyes are expressionless, windows into a stunned soul. His arm rises slowly and he presses his forefinger against the tip of Luis's nose like it's a button—a gesture from a memory still intact. I squeeze his hand hard. I hear myself say loud enough

for the driver to hear, "I've got your Lucky Strikes out in the car—
I'll go get them." Something like a smile forms at the edges of his
mouth, but soon fades into the slackness of his face.

"Don't you dare disappear," I whisper. "Don't you dare disappear
on me." I fight back the tears that have simply picked the wrong time
and place to reveal themselves.

I straighten up and say to the driver, "My car's parked down the
street—I'll just go out the back gate here."

"Why not?" He shrugs, not even looking up as he scribbles something official on the clipboard. He tucks it under his arm, then wheels
Henderson through the swinging doors.

For once the electric gate is open and I step out onto the sidewalk,
wide awake in broad daylight into Henderson's nighttime world.
Nothing looks familiar out here. Unlike Henderson, I don't have the
sleepwalker's flawless map. The sidewalk stretches out in front of
me. To anyone else who walks it every day it must seem a hard gray
line, but to me, the way the late afternoon light slants across it, it
holds a sheen like old silver. The lines spaced at regular intervals are
like the frets on the neck of a long guitar. Things sparkle in the cement
and even the shards of a broken green bottle near the curb shine,
luminous as emeralds.

Luis is heavy, but a manageable weight. His head keeps turning,
first front, then back, then front again. His right foot kicks me
gently, rhythmically, in the side.

I haven't been out in three years and they've torn down the last
of what would be familiar landmarks to me. The vacant lot that used
to be across the street is now a drive-through car wash, brushes
whirling like dervishes, its pavement slick with a froth of suds.

The traffic that streaks by blurs the street with color and when a
chartreuse fire engine the color of a French liqueur comes toward us,
both Luis and I stare, and our heads turn, pulled in its wake to watch
it disappear around a corner.

If the sky were green and two moons were rising in the east I
couldn't be more surprised. I see now that the world I've lived in for

the past decade is a small shelter, a cave set back from the street. And yet, as soon as I step outside the gate, the outside world takes me in. People pass. Some nod, some smile, some never meet my gaze, but no one stares as if I don't belong here. Their faces are limned in reddish light. If they had any idea how beautiful they looked they would stop right there in midstride and touch their hands to their foreheads, their noses, their eyes.

We come to a bus stop and I sit down at the bench to rest. A boy, ten or twelve—I can't seem to tell ages anymore—comes toward us carrying an enormous box by a handle. Sound comes from it, sound without music, several voices speaking in a rhythm that rises and falls like the strange syllables of a foreign language. When he passes, I can feel the vowels thrumming in my ribs, and then he's moving away, trailing sound behind him like a long scarf unfurling the length of the block. Luis pumps up and down in my arms, set into motion as if an internal switch has been thrown, and since there's no one else here for the moment, well, I can't help it, I just rock a little from side to side.

Before long a city bus pulls up and the doors open with a hydraulic hiss, a prehistoric sigh. "Where does this go?" I call to the driver. He answers but I can't hear above the traffic so I get on anyway.

"How much?" I ask.

"Senior citizens twenty-five cents," he says.

"What about him?" I ask, indicating Luis.

"The baby goes for free."

I panic. I don't have a purse with me, have stepped out into the world horribly unprepared. I grope in my pocket with my free hand and feel the disk of a quarter, the quarter I've carried for an emergency phone call I've never had to make. I produce my money and hand it over. He hands me back a transfer—my first transaction in the outside world. I'm beginning to feel competent again.

I hold Luis up to the window so he can see out and he slaps his hands against it, bracing himself as the bus begins to roll. Outside the window the city careens—rushing up and pulling away faster than I can focus, a fantastic sum of combined numbers, the defining decimals fallen away.

A large expanse of green comes at us—Prospect Park, maybe. I reach up out of old habit without looking and pull the wire. The bell rings, the driver responds, the bus rolls to a stop. The door opens— all because I gave the right signal, am still fluent in the language of the realm.

As we enter the park, both of us stare at the flashes of color swinging or whirling around. I know it's a playground. To him it's something bright, moving. It's familiar, but dizzying, and I feel a nostalgia for the present even though I'm right in the middle of it. There's an hour or less left of light and when night falls I won't be going back to one of those brownstones along the park, hanging my coat on a particular hook in the hall closet, running water from the tap into a teakettle, drinking from a chipped but favorite cup— habits that could wear the grain right out of solid wood. What belongs to me now is what I can see in front of me for the short time I'm here—rough, unsanded, marvelous in all its textures. The river of noise and motion parts slightly to include me and I sail, oars up, with the capricious tide. I've always scoffed at the idea of magic. But the world out here has everything up its sleeve and pro- duces coins, pigeons, bouquets without flourish, one right after the other, whether one is paying attention or not. The very least I can do is look.

Rows of women sit on the benches, bringing their heads close together to murmur, turning occasionally to watch their children. These children play on the swings, climb in the jungle gym, and some, braver than I ever was, slide backward down the slide.

I sit on a bench with a black woman of middle age in a heavy blue coat. There are no black children playing so I figure she must be watching someone else's.

Two little girls, one slightly older than the other, are fighting over which way to face in the swing. The younger one wants to face the meadow in back, the older one insists that the right way is to face the sandbox. The woman at the other end of our bench leans forward and gestures with a red-mittened hand. "Sally, you let her do it the way she wants to. Her mind made up and you won't unmake it for her." Sally looks sullen for a moment. Her lips tighten to a fine line and her eyes narrow with the calculation of the next, more subtle assault.

The woman shakes her head and shrugs the coat closer around her. "Nobody seem able to leave anyone else alone in this world for two minutes at a time." She stuffs her hand back in her other pocket, her body symmetrical and round again. She eyes me. "That your grandchild?" She doesn't wait for an answer but nods assent. I'm obviously too old to be either mother or sitter.

"Want to hold him?" I ask her. We both lean closer to the middle of the bench for the exchange, then lean back again. Luis sits there on the broad blue lap, pulling at the red mittens that clasp him around his chest. She holds him a while, dancing him on her knees, then passes him back to me as if I were a place he belonged to.

"That one's built to last," she says, indicating the sturdy child who again leans against my chest. I support him lightly with my arms, which is unnecessary but I like the feel of him, warm inside the cold circle of my bones.

For a moment, as we sit there balanced on either end of the bench like a seesaw I think of Luis as part of my family reaching from a great distance, the son of my own nameless son or daughter, a direct line from an unknown place coming straight at me.

The arguments of the children on the swings blur into pure sound, the edges of words filed away. Their bright coats are patches of color, the leaves of trees are green shapes with flecks of blue or quivering gold between. My lap is warm, our breath becomes visible—three clouds of human atmosphere in the quickly cooling air.

Luis begins to squirm in my lap and before long he starts to cry.

"That boy's hungry—better get him home," says the woman, recognizing the signs so obvious to her, still foreign to me. She gets up to leave and we say good-bye, heading in opposite directions. When

I turn again I see her shape in the distance, navigating a familiar route home with the two girls firmly in hand.

I'm stiff from sitting so long in the open air. My hip aches but at least Luis is quiet again, distracted with motion. I make my way toward the park entrance but have to rest on a bench by the gate. A police officer comes toward me, his radio crackling indecipherable messages.

"Are you all right?" he asks, peering at my face in the dusk. His face is as round and pale as the moon as he bends close to me.

I nod. And it doesn't seem like capitulation to ask for help, just another simple transaction, so I say, "I guess we need a ride—I don't have money for the bus. We're from the Tender Loveing Care Home." It sounds as ridiculous spoken as it looks on the sign.

Luis and I get in the back of the police car. Home for us is two separate places, wards for the extremes of age. Luis begins to whimper again, softly this time with the patience that comes from experience with waiting, which already in his short life he has had. I'm back in my body again with all its persistent, inevitable betrayals, its makeshift mendings. Ahead of us, the lights of the Home blaze in their windows, the whole place alert and awake as we pull into the long, circular drive.

"Can you turn the red lights on—just for a minute?" I say as loudly as I can through the plastic shield that separates the front from the back.

He looks at me like I'm a prisoner with a last request. "Sure, why not—give 'em something to talk about."

The red and blue lights flash on top of the black and white car, sweeping across the front door of the Home, racing along the brick wall, even up to the second-story windows where faces appear one at a time. The officer opens the door for me and holds out his hand. I accept it and step into the swirling light, Luis perched on my good hip, as gracefully as I can manage. In the few seconds before Mrs. Valenzuela rushes down the front stairs I stand there in the center of concern and attention, in the brief awe I have coming to me. Tomorrow I will be fully returned, the subject of gossip and criticism, and closely watched from now on. But tonight I am close enough to danger to be fascinating, and I have news from another world.

Mrs. Valenzuela, to her great credit, does not snatch Luis from me but stands at a respectful distance and simply holds out her arms, her face calm and waiting. I take a step toward her in my own time and I hold him out in the space between us like a gift that finally must be given. I make sure she has him firmly before I let go.

❖ The lights are turned out, the murmuring in the hallway stops. I sit at the window and watch the moonlight move across the lawn until everything—the bench, the chinaberry tree, the circular walk—is gilded with it. So much more interesting to look at than my small space with its overstuffed chair and framed oval picture of my grandfather, the only adornments in a beige institutional room. Cautiously, I open the door and close it behind me. I make my way down the hall to the dayroom.

Henderson's by the window, smoking a cigarette. I sit down across from him and neither of us speak for a minute. At our feet are shadows of trees like a charcoal drawing on a sketchbook page. "It's Althea," I say.

"Yes," he says, "I know." He takes another puff. "What was it like out there?" he asks, looking over his shoulder toward the window, indicating places beyond its view.

I think for a moment, bringing it back to me. I think of Luis, how it must have looked to him, how it looked to me, joined to him in the confluence of sight. And I think of Vera too and what she might say if she could suddenly see. "*You* know. It was bright. And fast, very fast, and I couldn't get enough of it in a single afternoon."

Henderson nods and reaches into his bathrobe pocket, his hand finding something that crackles with cellophane.

"Want a smoke, Althea? Lucky Strikes—the best."

He shakes the pack in a movement made perfect by practice. I take a cigarette and he leans toward me in the dark, flipping back the metal cap of the Zippo lighter. I lean toward him, like a baby reaching for the moon before the mind believes in distance. My hand is shaking.

"Some things still taste good," he says, whispering smoke into the air.

I nod in assent, the forbidden cigarette between my lips. Its tip flares with the draw of my breath and it bobs up and down, a tiny signal flare, answering.

❖ *Procession*

I no longer remember how we broke into the church, or why. But it was late August, a still point between seasons, and my cousin and I were nearly twelve and restless and out of ideas on how to fill the long, humid days. We were tomboys. Dolls didn't hold our attention, and the miniature golf course where we spent our afternoons was closed for maintenance or remodeling. The streets of Bethlehem, Pennsylvania, were all too familiar to us—we could ride our bikes through them blindfolded. The steel mill was going to lay off come fall—both our fathers could feel it coming—and with that edginess in the air my cousin Laura and I felt compelled to do something that had always scared us.

The Catholic church loomed over the low houses that surrounded it. This was Protestant country—Moravian—and even the building seemed foreign, though it was made of the same bricks as every other denomination. We rode our bikes around and around its circular driveway, and then we stopped, laid them down on the lawn at the side of the church. The colored streamers from our handlebars lay limp and mixed in with the tangle of grass and clover. We looked at the friary where everyone said the monks lived, at the cross and the steeple, but the familiar symbol of the cross seemed as lofty as the flag from an unpronounceable country. We were, after all, Presbyterians and wary of what people referred to as papists, but we were drawn to this place, to the mystery it surely contained and protected.

It seemed quite natural that the doors were locked to us, that we had to break something—a lock, a pane of glass (I can remember the sound, but can't see it shattered at my feet). It was a basement door we chose to violate and it opened into a maw of damp and darkness. We walked blindly through it, our arms tense, outstretched, the soles of our rubber tennis shoes catching on the rough concrete floor. My foot hit something that clanged as hollow as a bell. I held out my hands to describe its shape—a bucket, cold and round, and inside it a dry string mop, its handle broken off, the mop head feeling for all the world as stiff as if it had been starched, frozen into curls.

"Watch it, for Chrissakes," Laura hissed at me. I'd never heard her swear before. The phrase "using the Lord's name in vain" came to me, and I thought it meant that he wouldn't hear it no matter how loud you were.

"Well, shit," I said, and felt a satisfaction like the first time I spit on the sidewalk or lit a match beneath my bedspread late at night to take a single, choking, delicious draw on one of my father's Chesterfields.

We moved forward until we came to a wall, then felt our way along the seams of bricks. Our hands, if we could have seen them, would have been pocked from the rough surface.

Laura found a door, and this one was not locked. It opened easily, without sound, onto a narrow wooden staircase winding up to the floor above us. Light came down the shaft like sunlight pointing deep into a well. I went first and climbed until I came to a heavy velvet curtain that covered the entrance to the stairs. I peered around it

quickly but waited for Laura before I really looked—I didn't want
to see it by myself, whatever it was.

The curtain we stood behind hung at the side of the altar, and
when we looked around it we saw a place that would upstage anyone standing in it: significant light streamed through leaded glass
from high-up windows, and the altar dripped with white brocade
and gold braid and a hundred burning candles. Above the altar hung
a bloody Christ, pierced and skinny and sad. But even he was over-
shadowed by his mother—a statue of Mary stood to the side, looming blue and unearthly, pale with virginity and grace.

Everything was familiar but strange in a way that made our
own faith seem shortchanged. Our church, with its hard wooden
benches, a table with a cross on a low pedestal, seemed mean and
crude, with nothing to distract or hush you during the endless ser-
mon and drone of hymns. Here, a veil of incense drifted through the
air, candles wavered in ruby-colored glass. I wondered where the
friars were who lit them. Did they use lighters or special matches?
Did they sing in here or were there only murmurs and prayers?

I'd seen a rosary once—Carla Hernandez at school had one. All I
knew is I wanted one too, now that I'd seen the rest of it, the place
you knelt in, holding it, counting your way to forgiveness.

If we had gone in with ideas of doing damage we had forgotten
them now. Laura didn't swear anymore and I couldn't see anything
I wanted to steal or leave my mark on. I felt like pretending to be
Catholic, to cross myself and curtsy though I didn't know if you went
from right to left or the other way around—it seemed important to
get it right or not do it at all. We were both afraid to step out into
the field of vision of the statues or the scrutiny of their God who
stared at us through the stained glass. So we just stood there in the
shelter of the curtain, our heads uncovered, our hair hanging long
and wild from riding through the humid wind.

Laura pointed to a door at the left of the altar. I nodded. We were
outside of language, reduced to signs, gestures. We tiptoed like thieves
across the red carpet and as we passed in front of the altar, I couldn't

stop myself—I took one of the candles in the glass cups, the glass hot and warm, the wick nearly burned down to the metal tab that anchored it in a pool of thick, creamy wax.

Then we couldn't get through the door fast enough—I ran past her and into the room on the other side of that door and stopped, struggling for balance from the shock of what I had entered into. The low-ceilinged room was dim and smoky, not with incense, but with the smoke of cigarettes held casually in the hands of at least a dozen friars not twenty feet away. Their cowls were pushed back, their brown uniformity broken by the different colored sportshirts they wore underneath. Several wore glasses, some were losing their hair, one was in his stockinged feet. They had not seen us yet—they were absorbed in conversation. They sat in folding chairs, not in orderly rows, but at random, though there was an aisle of sorts through them. At the end of that aisle we could see the red EXIT sign over a door.

One of them looked up suddenly, then they all stopped talking and turned toward us. Smoke curled from their fingers as if escaping from a fissure beneath which something smoldered and burned. Someone exhaled carefully, almost thoughtfully, and a ring of smoke hovered in the air.

There seemed no choice but to move forward. I walked toward them, still holding the candle, and I felt Laura follow behind me. I moved closer to them, as if I had a perfect right to be there, as if they were waiting for me to pass.

All their eyes were on me and I felt them search my face for something I could not show them. I walked past the first man, and then another. I felt their breath, warm with smoke, clouding toward me. Their feet were ordinary beneath the graceful, deep folds of their robes. I did not see faces, only feet on the beige linoleum floor, in a variety of common shoes. Once I noticed a hand on a knee, a wrist-watch with a luminous dial, the second hand sweeping.

The votive candle was hot in my hands and I wanted to drop it, but I knew I no longer had that choice. I had to hold on, had to walk all the way through without stopping. I believed I held something magic between my palms, that they knew it, and that's why they let me pass. If I dropped it, the spell would be broken—someone would speak and I would have to answer, Laura and I would have to be caught, or run.

I approached the last man, the candle searing my skin. Something made me pause, he seemed about to speak and I looked right at him, waiting. His glasses were in his hand. There were deep red indentations where they had been resting on the bridge of his nose. I imagined myself through nearsighted eyes—a blurred figure with a flare of light cupped in her hands. He reached out toward me and his fingers felt the air, inches from my own. Slowly, he brought the glasses closer to his face and his eyes grew magnified, huge and strange and exposed. They blinked once and half the wonder went out of them as a smile crept in. He reached toward me but this time I moved away. I made myself keep walking slowly until Laura was past him too. Then my hand was on the cool brass doorknob, turning it, pushing it out and open. As we stepped through I could imagine how their stunned silence would end as soon as I closed the door, how someone might laugh, or be indignant, or angry. I could see our bikes on the grass not so very far away. I pulled the door closed. I dropped the candle. It did not break, but rolled into the grass and went out.

We broke into a run, we ran for our lives though we knew we were not in any danger, that they would not follow or question or scold us. It seemed we could no longer be punished or forgiven. I looked at Laura as we rode away but she avoided my eyes. I knew we would not speak of it, then or ever. I pedaled hard. The wind filled my skirt and lifted my hair, and what I wanted then, what I would always want, was to tell, just to tell someone.

❖ *Lake Effect*

It was the monsoon that started it, that gave her the idea of being thoroughly drenched as a way of coming clean. She saw the cumulus clouds building to the south and lay down on the parched Bermuda grass to wait.

When it came, the drops of rain were so huge they hurt, but Lorna stretched her arms and legs out in the gradually forming mud—like a snow angel. She felt her skin open and it was as satisfying as sex at an unexpected time of day.

Which made her think even more about Ray, up on the Flathead Reservation in Montana, swimming naked in a lake, kissing his ex-wife's breasts underwater. She hoped he ran out of breath.

The sun came out and heated the drops of water on her face. The sun drilled into the top of her head, heated her earrings until they burned the skin on her neck. The mud dried quickly, encasing her fingers in a brown, thin sheath that cracked when she moved. The rain wasn't nearly enough. She had a sudden urge to stand waist deep in the ocean, to feel the cool spray sheared off the waves, to taste salt not of her own making. She needed to get out of the house. The place was like a tomb since Ray left a week ago. The night he left she'd found a scorpion on the bathroom ceiling—had to thwack it down with the toilet plunger. That was the last straw. Even her own zodiac sign was mocking her.

❖ She followed the sunset for a while, wished she could keep pace with it, but just east of Quartzsite she lost the light and the sky was as pitch black as the asphalt under her until the moon finally rose. She only stopped once all the way to San Diego and only then because she ran out of gas near Twenty-nine Palms. The delay was brief. She had a full jerry can of gas in the back and soon she was in high gear again. She didn't eat and only took occasional sips of water from a canteen next to her on the seat. Her Toyota pickup's steady fifth-gear hum etched itself deeply in her eardrums like a percussion track and she heard it long after she shut the engine down near La Jolla at dawn. And there she was, finally, at the edge of the country, ready to see the Pacific, except the Pacific had disappeared, been swallowed up by such a dense, implacable fog that even the waves seemed ironed flat.

Lorna stood in the sand barefoot, wired with adrenalin and furious, her neck muscles locked in spasm from the drive. She went in the water anyway, waded out in her shorts and T-shirt. She tested the time-worn cliché and held her hand in front of her face. She could see it, but it looked vague and disembodied, like the hand of someone else reaching out to stop her.

Back at the truck she wrapped herself in a towel, then got behind the wheel again. She could hardly stand to take hold of it anymore, felt the stickiness her sweaty palms had left there. But she headed north, determined to find a break in the fog.

A 7-Eleven loomed out of nowhere and at its entrance a figure in a hooded sweatshirt held a sign out toward her as she passed. Will Work for Food, it said. She'd seen that sign many times in Tucson.

She drove by, craning her neck to get a better look. He was old enough to be somebody's grandfather, but still ... She pulled over a quarter mile down the road and watched in the rearview mirror as he turned slowly around. He didn't move after that, just stood there, the sign dangling from his right hand, touching the ground. She had the eerie feeling he could see her eyes in the mirror, though that was impossible. There was something so resigned about the way he stood, a take-it-or-leave-it posture, beyond disappointment. In her present mood, it annoyed her. But there was also something about it that made her curious—he seemed too patient to be threatening. She put the truck in reverse and backed up along the shoulder; he got larger and larger in the mirror. She locked the passenger door as she pulled up alongside him, but rolled down the window halfway. The hooded shape leaned down and she could see a white beard, a pair of dark eyes behind wire-rimmed glasses, a face lined like a topographical map. His fingers rested lightly on the window. She lowered it the rest of the way and his hands went down with it.

"Is that sign true?"

He looked at her in surprise and dismay. "Of course it's true— I wrote it myself."

"Well, the only reason I ask is I've stopped before and sometimes people hold up that sign because they want you to just give them the money and then leave them alone."

"Well I plan to work, like it says." He straightened up slightly, as if he half expected her to drive off any second without warning.

"What kind of work can you do?" She really wanted to know. The words on the sign, since he meant them, seemed more personal than the most desperate of personal ads.

"Gardening, hauling." He stopped for a minute, as if trying to remember. "Tuning the engines of American cars. Ironing."

She pictured him ironing an endless pile of someone else's shirts, meticulously working the tip of the iron around each button.

"Can you drive?"

"Certainly." He looked slightly offended.

"Can you drive me north a ways—I'm dead tired—I've been driving all night from Tucson. I'll buy lunch on the way."

"Well yes, I could do that." He nodded solemnly, as if to seal the bargain.

Lorna slid over the seat and he got in carefully on the driver's side. He ran his hand across the dashboard, leaving a dark trail in the brown coat of dust.

"It's different—everything's different. Last truck I owned was a '51 Ford." He pulled his hood down. His white hair nearly grazed the ceiling. "The world is getting smaller."

"Buckle your seatbelt," Lorna said.

He felt along the seat cushion behind him.

"It's over your left shoulder these days."

He stretched it across his chest, staring at it before he clicked it into place. "Good God," he said.

The gearshift was familiar to him and he went through all four easily with only a slight buck in first; he left the fifth alone.

He relaxed once they were moving. "Name's Fenway," he said. "You?"

"Lorna. What's Fenway for?"

"Like the ballpark—you know, in Boston. My father picked it out when my mother died. I believe she would have called me Thomas."

"I like Fenway better."

She leaned her head against the window. The dunes blurred into a single, sandy streak. She closed her eyes.

"Stop at the first place you see a break in this damn fog," she told him.

"Well, that might be a while."

"I'm not in that much of a hurry."

Lorna thought about trying to sleep, but she just couldn't close her eyes. She was aware of him there, not two feet away. She wondered if she was any judge of character any more. She had been dead wrong about Ray, which surprised at least as much as it hurt her. When she met him, it had been three years since her divorce. It had been enough time, she thought, to see straight again, but at thirty-nine, so much was at stake—even sex was not a simple pleasure any longer. Ray seemed as solid as a tree at first, but soon after they'd begun to spend time together he'd become like St. Elmo's fire, burning without specific heat. She thought if she could just get away somewhere with water and stay in that water long enough she could be washed clean of his feel, his smell, his harm, that bad taste of her own mistake.

She heard a tapping sound and turned her head to see Fenway rapping the Plexiglas face of the fuel gauge with his finger as if it were an old watch that needed coaxing. He peered at it and then she felt the truck lurching on the last of the fumes. Damn. She'd forgotten to tell him the gauge didn't work, that it stayed on half a tank forever no matter how full or empty it was.

He steered for the shoulder and the truck rolled slowly like a toy winding down until it stopped completely. The generator light flashed on.

Fenway looked at her. "Dry as a bone," he said, not as an accusation but as a statement of fact.

"There's a five-gallon can in the back—"

"Now that's planning ahead."

"But I used it up the last time I ran out, near Twenty-nine Palms."

"Well then." He set the parking brake, jerked it hard until it caught. "I never drove anywhere without extra."

"I don't need a lecture, I just need some gas."

He glared at her, then opened the door, swung himself out and lifted the empty jerry can.

"Look, I've just had a hard time lately and my manners have gone out the window. I'd appreciate it if you'd get some gas—I'll throw in an extra meal."

He relaxed, but only slightly. "About a mile back there's a Texaco."

Lorna nodded, reached into her cut-offs and uncrumpled a twenty-dollar bill. She had nothing smaller and regretted it. She handed it to him and for half a second they each held an end in their fingers, a paper bridge between them.

"Unleaded," she said.

She wondered if she would ever see him or her money again, wondered how long he could live on it. Would he be extravagant and blow it on a bottle and a steak, or parcel it out in frugal meals over a week's time?

"I'll be back in an hour, less if I get a ride."

She nodded her head, then scrunched down in the seat to sleep, but before she closed her eyes she watched him recede in the side mirror, a man with a limp trudging toward the vanishing point of the road.

❖ She woke to the irregular cadence of his footsteps coming, gravel crunching beneath his shoes. She heard the sound of the gas can emptying and the tank drinking fuel in huge gulps. Before he got back in the truck he handed her change through the window.

"You've earned yourself several meals, Fenway." She took the money.

"I'd like the first one as soon as possible."

"You choose a place then."

Before they'd gone even ten miles, Fenway pulled into the parking lot of a building shaped like a lighthouse with Edna's Fish and Chips painted on the curved wall. They sat at a formica table in unmatched metal kitchen chairs next to an aquarium teeming with Halloween-colored fish.

Fenway ordered the Captain's Plate, Lorna the Small Fry. Both orders came wrapped in Sunday's edition of the *San Diego Union*. Fenway shook vinegar all over his chips but left the fish alone. He ate carefully, almost thoughtfully, considering each bite. Lorna devoured hers in no time.

He began to talk between bites.

"Last real job I had was a one-week stint on the Golden Gate Bridge, setting up those orange cones to make more lanes, going north at night, south in the morning. I rode in a little jump seat close to the ground on the back of a truck and swung my arm out to set the cones in place. There was a rhythm to it if you did it right, but sometimes the cars coming the other way would nearly take your arm off."

"I hope they paid well. How old are you anyway? I'd think they would only let someone younger do that kind of work."

"I'm sixty-two." He shook more vinegar on the chips. "And not retired. You know, I kept thinking of the man whose job I was doing while he was on vacation—Hawaii, they said—and I pitied him, leaving the blue water and the coconut palms to come back to that. I don't know how people can live that way, repeating themselves day in and day out."

He finished off the last piece of fish. "What about you—you work?"

"Well I don't have a boring job."

"What do you do?"

"I take care of the spiders at the Desert Museum."

"Can't they take care of themselves?"

"Well up to a point. I still have to feed them. But mostly I work with school groups that come through, bring out the tarantulas so the kids can pet them."

"What do they feel like?"

"The best description I can give you is what a first-grade girl told me last week—she said it was like a little ballerina dancing on her hand."

Fenway shook his head. "It's been a long time since I was around any children. Never had any of my own. What about you?"

"Nope. Not married."

"Well why ever not?"

"I really couldn't say." She studied the newspaper in front of her, grease-blotched ads for lingerie at Sears. She used to think she'd end up marrying Ray. Until he ran, leaving a note behind that said nothing more than he was sorry, but he couldn't help it, he was going back to his wife. Next to the note, he'd left her extra set of keys—the ones she'd given him so he wouldn't feel like he was just a visitor in her home. She got his number from information once in Missoula, dialed it, got his answering machine. His message said, "Carol and I are not here right now to take your call, but leave a message as long as you like and one of us will get back to you just as soon as we can." Lorna's message said, "This won't take long. And I seriously doubt if you're going to get back to me just as soon as you can. I just want to know how you can stand to live with yourself anymore."

She rattled the ice around in her cup and stabbed the straw down in a new place, took a pull on it.

She looked up at the clock on the wall. Three o'clock, neither lunch nor dinner.

"You still hungry—you want another order?" She didn't like being focused on. Anyway, she could hardly explain it to him when she hadn't made sense of it herself.

"I could eat another and still be comfortable. Yes I could. If not, then I'll just take it with me."

"When did you last eat, Fenway?"

He thought a minute.

"Tuesday."

It was Friday.

❖ The second order came wrapped in the want ads. He scanned them slowly while he ate.

Lorna watched him eat, and felt satisfaction from it. She tried to imagine him in a house, at a table, eating on a china plate with a real glass filled with ice water.

"Do you have a home?"

"Used to. Nebraska, outside of Grand Island."

"Well why aren't you still there?" She felt as self-conscious as if she were asking a man with one eye how he lost the other one.

"Repossessed. Pure and simple. Couldn't make the payments anymore. My wife Helen died—four years ago now—and after that I couldn't work, couldn't even mow the fields. I gave the dog away because I could hardly remember to feed it. After three months of that I knew that if I didn't start moving I'd just stop altogether."

She watched his hands, noted the swollen knuckles, the dark concentric whorls in his fingertips—years of work remembered in the skin.

"Where did you grow up, Lorna?"

"I was an army brat."

"That's tough on a kid."

"Yeah—different school for every year of high school: Fort Dix, Pendleton, Presidio."

"How'd you get to Arizona?"

"I picked it because it was no place my father had ever dragged me to. The first thing I did when I got my new address was to have it printed on envelope stickers—I planned on staying a long time."

They leaned back in the metal chairs. An occasional fly lighted on the table, fastened itself to a crumb. Lorna found it almost hard to imagine her house. She'd rarely felt at home there even though she loved its adobe walls, cool as a cave even in summer, the beamed ceilings and hardwood floors, the arched doorways that seemed a shape from another country.

She had just gotten used to living there alone and halfway liking it when she met Ray. He'd been camping out for a month on Mount Lemmon and was not particularly subtle about making it clear he needed a place to stay. She was wary at first, but found she liked the change he brought to the house. He loved to cook—Chinese food mostly—and the kitchen was filled with the sound of stir-frying, the heady scent of plum sauce, garlic, and soy. So different from the meals she'd made alone: instant noodles and scrambled eggs she usually ate standing up at the kitchen counter, right out of the pan. She was comfortable in the disorder of his clothes strewn over chairs along with hers, in the noise (he was always listening to African and Indonesian music), in the warm, human curve of another body next to hers and the lovely necessity of changing the sheets more than once a week. Ray had brought a cat he named Graffiti from the pound one day, and when it learned the house, it felt safe enough to sleep on top of the bed instead of under it, wedged between their legs. So the house looked like a lived-in home and felt like it too until the day he just disappeared.

She cleaned the house for days, sweeping up every last shred of evidence of his six-month stay, every last fleck of kitty litter on the tiled floor. Just when she was sure she'd gotten everything, she moved the couch to sweep beneath it and there, bright red and green and yellow, were the cat's rubber balls, batted beyond reach. She knew if she looked at them too long she'd just get pissed or sad or both, so she put them in a cardboard box along with the laundry he'd left in the hamper and the six-pack of beer he'd crammed in the refrigerator and, on her way out of town, stopped at a Goodwill box in a church parking lot on Speedway. She couldn't get the box in the small slot of the metal bin no matter how hard she pushed, couldn't get that satisfying thud she'd imagined when the box hit the bottom, so she just left it there, half in and half out, and drove away.

❖ Lorna sucked the last of her iced tea through the straw, stared at the mollies and angelfish swimming listlessly in the tank.

Fenway finished the last of his second order and said, "You seem like a person who spends a lot of time thinking."

"You could say that."

"Well your life can't be that hard to figure out—you're too young to be this complicated in your head already."

"Wanna bet? You've known me the short part of an afternoon and that's not long enough to read my mind."

He sat up straight, spread his hands flat on the table in front of him and leaned into them. His eyes fixed on her, but the way the light hit his glasses she could see only the windows reflected in them, the shape of herself there in shadow. "And you don't know me from Adam, young lady, any more than you knew whoever gave you such a hard time. All I know is where I am at the moment. Sixty-five miles north of San Diego. Right now I'm at Edna's Fish and Chips with a young lady from Arizona and we're discussing our losses. This might be my house." He threw his arm out to indicate the room. "And this could well be my own kitchen table here." He rapped on it with his knuckles. "And you might be a neighbor who's just lost her farm or her man or both and come to talk. And I'd make us a pot of coffee, never mind the time of day, and by dusk you might get around to saying something honest and I might say something you'd remember that would help you home. I'd tell you you're a beautiful woman and someone will come along one day that won't be able to forget you."

Her face felt hot. She couldn't look at him. What the hell was he talking about? She studied her lap and tried to feel herself in a farmhouse kitchen with a friend, with the sky going lavender and the fields turned to blond. In the kitchen Edna dumped a load of raw potatoes into a frying vat and their sizzle sounded like a downpour on a tin roof. When Lorna finally looked at him he was dipping his fingers into the aquarium, so slowly the fish were grouped together, transfixed by the fleshy shape that had entered into their world. He flicked his fingers once and they shot away.

❖ Fenway pulled the truck back onto the coast highway. If anything, the fog was thicker, wetter.

"You might have to settle on a lake today if you still want to go swimming. Big Bear's the closest."

Lorna looked at the fog-veiled coast. The whole idea of coming here seemed impetuous and irrational, though she appreciated the fact that Fenway didn't say so.

"A lake will do fine."

He headed east, drove in silence for several miles.

She wanted to talk or, at least, to keep on listening to him. "What's the strangest place you've ever been, Fenway?"

"I once hitched to Alaska when those whales were stuck in the ice—saw it on TV in a truck stop in Spokane. I just thought I ought to try to be there, even if it didn't make much sense to go to that kind of trouble to save two when we'd wiped out thousands of their relatives."

"Did you make it in time?"

"Yes I did, and I stayed up seventy-two hours straight when I got there, breaking up the ice with a metal rod. Mustache froze solid from all the coffee it dipped into. When the whales finally got free, and all those newspeople were running around in their brand-new L. L. Bean togs, I just waved my watch cap in the air—I'll never forget the sight of them going out that channel. It was worth it, absolutely."

She stole a glance at his face, imagining the frozen mustache as if it was the cold that turned it white.

"It was better than seeing God, as far as I'm concerned. Even after the whales showed themselves, they were still a mystery."

❖ The sun finally broke through the low clouds an hour inland and grew stronger as they drove upward through the mountains. Big Bear Lake was nearly empty when they pulled into a campsite by the shore. Tall pines grew to the edge of the rocky shoreline. There was a little strip of sand by their campsite—a semblance of a beach. A few midweek fishermen drifted slowly in wooden boats far out on the water. The sun shone, unimpeded by clouds, and the lake rippled like liquid silver when the breeze stirred its surface.

"Did you bring a swimsuit?"

She thought a minute, then laughed. "Guess not."

She waded in in her shorts and T-shirt and felt the lovely rising coolness coming to her by degrees. She stopped when it reached her shoulders and then she let herself sink down all the way. She opened her eyes and found herself in a green place woven through with yellow straws of light, the bottom invisible, the sky a bright lens overhead. She felt her hair stream out behind her as she swam. She thought of making love with Ray, how it was always languid but silent in a way that unsettled her—he never made a sound until it was over. So many times she'd wanted to stop, ask him something, just to hear his voice in the dark. She ran out of breath before she wanted to, and surfaced, facing the middle of the lake. She treaded water for a while, watched the boats drift, then turned herself around. She felt cleaner, stronger as she stroked her way through the water.

She couldn't see Fenway anywhere and felt a clench of panic as sudden as a cramp. She started running when she was still waist-deep in water and it was like running in a dream, leaden and bullied by gravity. She sloshed up onto the narrow strip of sandy beach, her clothes dripping lake water down her legs. She stood there shivering, despite the sun.

"Fenway?" she called.

Jays shrieked in the trees, the sound of an outboard motor started up somewhere across the lake.

"Fenway!" she shouted, surprised at her voice, how loud it could be when it needed to be.

Nothing. She looked in the truck. The keys were gone.

She paced up and down the beach for a time then made herself sit down on the picnic table to dry off, but the bench was so hot it burned the backs of her thighs and she jumped right up again.

"Sonofabitch! You sonofabitch!" She was screaming at the top of her lungs now, she didn't care who else heard her. She pounded on the sticky table. "Give me back my keys!"

She stalked up and down the beach, kicking at the water, sending up sprays of water. "You always learn the hard way, don't you, Lorna?" she said out loud, like a parent to a twice-told child. She was so furious she didn't hear him come back, but did hear the sound of the keys hitting the picnic table.

She stood there, ankle-deep, dripping, glaring at him.

"I will not be taken advantage of anymore, especially by you!" She stomped her foot and sent a shower of water in his direction.

"I'm not young enough to take advantage of anyone anymore. I'm the least of your worries. I wasn't making off with your keys— I forgot I had them. Went looking for the showers. Found 'em, too." He pushed back his hair and she could see that it was wet.

She felt so surprised she didn't know what to say.

"Besides, I don't have any intention of running out on somebody who still owes me a meal."

Slowly, her mouth worked itself into a grin.

❖ Shopping with Fenway was an experience. He examined each pepper, onion, and potato as if they were the first of their kind he'd ever had the privilege to see and when she ordered two steaks at the butcher counter he took the paper-wrapped package from her carefully like a breakable gift. He lifted their purchases one at a time onto the checkout counter and told the bagger to pack things carefully so the bag of charcoal wouldn't bruise the apples.

Back at the lake, Fenway started a fire in the grill using pine needles and twigs as kindling. He bent his body to blow his breath on the needles until they caught the flame and held it, then he fed it steadily until he had a bed of coals to lay the charcoal on.

Lorna had a pocketknife in the truck and chopped the peppers and onions in half, trimmed the steak of excess fat, and rubbed the vegetables with it. Fenway carried it all over to the fire and laid it, a piece at a time, onto the hot tines of the grill. The meat spit and sizzled, the onions smoked and browned, the peppers curled and softened. The water reflected the sunset, pink and gold, without ripples. The wind had died down and there was no sound but the cooking of meat, the last cries of birds as they headed for their roosts in the trees. A nearly full moon rose, backlighting the jagged edges of the pines at the far end of the lake. Lorna opened a carton of lemonade and they passed it back and forth to each other.

When the food was cooked they piled it onto paper plates and set to, spearing pieces with opened jackknives, juice running into their palms.

Neither of them said a word.

Lorna took her time, chewed everything completely. There was no hurry. She knew that when they finished, they would leave, and she would drop him off at some junction. He'd hold the sign in his hands and someone else would eventually take him seriously for the next meal and maybe the one after that. And she knew she would drive east through desert, through long stretches of interstate without lights, and that the next time she sat down in her own kitchen everything she did there would remind her of this, how they ate, how they rose from the table, satisfied, how they walked down to the lake afterward, and when she cupped the water to wash, how the moon wavered in her hands.

❖ *Communiqué*

It seemed to her that it always worked before—an unfamiliar destination, long talks in dark stretches of highway between exits, journal entries written in cafes for a book they might collaborate on one day—it all led to making love in strange rooms where they were closer together because they were nowhere they'd ever been.

Last night, at the end of such a journey, they sat on the cabin floor as the fire he'd built, barely contained in the cast-iron stove, threw sparks that landed harmlessly on the tiled hearth before them. She held his hand and could feel the change in him as if even the blood in his veins moved differently. He was *letting* her hold his hand—her own hand was not specifically held. He was silent, too, and seemed as strange to her as the place they had come to where the water looked as black as oil in the moonless night and the houses that crouched over the bay on stilts seemed tentative, as if they knew their foundations were eaten away a little more with each high tide.

He did not look at her as she undressed though the first time he saw her that way she had felt the sudden warmth as he pulled her close, the quick, following coolness of his tears on her skin. Now she stood there, chilled, not five feet from the fire, her clothes in a heap on the floor. She felt utterly stranded. Alone. And something else: ashamed, her nakedness blatant and uninvited. A new word came to her. A word not in the vocabulary of their intimacy. There was no other word for it—that ancient insult of sudden indifference: she felt spurned.

❖ She listens at the door. There is safety in the sound of running water, the steady percussion of it in the porcelain tub, the fall of water impeded only by his body. She can tell when he rinses the shampoo from his hair—the water makes a cascading sound then—and she knows she still has time because he always lathers twice.

She opens his briefcase, stares at the journal lying on top of a pile of papers. The fact that he kept one fascinated her. What did he keep in there—dreams, mileage records, field notes for his job as a geologist, comments on things he'd read? She argues with herself about opening it. But it's not idle curiosity. It seems the only place to either confirm her fears or put them to rest. Either way, she needs to know.

She finds the last entry, dated two days ago. She reads, "I'm uncomfortable with her intensity and it feels more all the time like she's clinging." Her heart sounds louder than the drumming of the water on the metal shower stall.

She turns back to the entry dated the day after they met, six months ago. "Couldn't sleep. I've been thinking about her all night—the way her hands moved when she talked and how those same hands will touch me. This may seem crazy to say so, but I think she's someone I could spend a long time with."

This surprises her. He's had a string of relationships that didn't last more than a year. He always talked about how much he needed his solitude and seemed intent on protecting it at all costs.

She closes the journal, puts it back. How could the first entry about her be so completely edited out by the last?

She wants to rip the page from its perfect binding, burn it in the fireplace of the cabin they rented for a hundred dollars for a single night and did not make love in. Or, better yet, take her English teacher's red pen, circle that insulting, niggardly word "clinging" and write hugely in the margin, "Substantiate!" But it's not something he's handed in for a grade. She has, after all, broken a cardinal rule. Journals are sacred, although she feels justified now that she knows directly he has not told her the truth of what he feels.

The water stops. She puts on her coat and walks out of the dark, musty, overpriced cabin and heads for the sunlight just showing at the edge of the meadow. She doesn't want to be there waiting when he comes out of the bathroom. She wants him to feel, for a moment, the stillness of a strange place, to be alone and vaguely uneasy.

She makes a wide circle around the meadow. Her sneakers turn dark, wet with dew, and her pants are soon studded with burdock. She walks with her fists clenched and suddenly she stops, opens her mouth to wail, but it comes out more like a yell, a deep sound, like an animal, and for half a second that pleases her, that there is something simple, primal, an ancient spring of wrath, that she has finally tapped into. But it is, after all, a furtive sound, despite its volume, a solitary utterance in an open field.

This is what's familiar to her—this walking in a silent, heated rage, her mouth sealed against itself. Once, when she was five or six, her mother overheard her talk back to her father for pinching her too hard. Her mother said, "Don't you dare speak to your father like that—now you march right back in there and apologize." But she couldn't do it. She stood there just outside his study, shifting from one foot to the other, unable to say she was sorry when she wasn't. *He* should be the one apologizing. Her mother found her and marched her downstairs to the unfinished rec room and told her to stay down there until she felt good and sorry. And she did feel sorry—not for what she'd said, but for the fact that she'd said it loud enough for him to hear. All she could hear was the muffled laugh track of the Jackie Gleason show and, during the commercials, the heavy footsteps of her parents on the wooden floor above her.

She retraces her steps. The burdock on her jeans is so thick it feels like armor. She is a plant with sharp edges, protected as cactus.

He is sitting on the bed when she opens the door. His hair is wet, stringy, the blond turned to dun. His receding hairline is obvious. She finds satisfaction in this image—he is unattractive at this moment —a balance to the image he must have had of her to assign that word to her. Clinging. She imagines a child, wailing to be picked up, a towering adult who won't come near it.

He looks up from the Sunday paper he's reading. "Hi," he says, and smiles.

"Hi," she says and keeps on going, straight into the bathroom that is as dank and sweaty as a cave. The mirror is so fogged her face does not even register as a blur. She turns on the water in the sink and brushes her teeth furiously, spitting over and over again the word, the terrible word, the mean sound of it that reminds her of its synonym and ugly sister, "cloying."

She shuts off the water, polishes a circle in the mirror—a cameo, hard as ivory, the body below the neck invisible. She is ready. She turns the doorknob and it comes off immediately in her hand. She looks at it in disbelief.

She pounds on the door. "Hey!" she shouts, and hears the accusation in her tone, as if he's the one who's locked her in.

She bangs louder. What if he's gone for a walk?

He comes to the door, laughing. "Let's see now," he says through the door. "What do I want from you? What'll you give me if I let you out?"

"You've already gotten everything," she says, surprising herself.

He opens the door. She looks at him with a level stare, then walks past him into the room. He's not laughing now, but he didn't get it either. He just looks confused.

She sits on the edge of the bed. He leans against the dresser. There's a mirror behind him and she can see both the front and the back of him all at once.

"Find anything interesting out there?" he asks.

She picks at the burdock stuck to her jeans. "Yeah, I guess. There's a meadow just behind that line of trees." She glances out the window once, then concentrates on the growing pile of stickers at her feet. She picks up a book that lies splayed on the bed to mark his place.

"What did you think?"

"Classic American stories, in the great tradition of the desire to be elsewhere: mill towns closing down, stolen cars, people stunned with the idea of where they might get to if they drive long enough."

She thumbs through the first few pages to the table of contents, recognizes the title of a story she'd assigned to her class from an anthology of contemporary writers. She remembers liking it, but remembers some controversy in the class discussion, something about the female characters, though she can't remember what.

Her eyes travel across the room to his briefcase. The journal is inside. She wonders if he knows she looked. Had she put it back upside down in an unconscious gesture to leave a trail he could trace to her? But he seems annoyingly innocent right now.

She feels like provoking him, doesn't want to agree with him on anything, no matter how trivial.

"He doesn't know how to write about women."

"Why? They seemed accurately portrayed to me."

"They're what men fantasize about women—women who don't need anything from them."

"Well that's a sweeping generalization—you'd never let me get away with that."

She stands up, agitated, walks over to the In-Room coffeepot mounted on the wall. She tears open the packet of instant coffee, shakes it into a cup, flips the switch under the tiny pot of water. A yellow light comes on, an electric hum emanates from the wall. The hot plate ticks, expanding with heat.

"That woman in the first story should have gotten on a bus, but no—she just sat there, driving deeper into trouble with a thief!"

"You're talking plot now, not character. She had nowhere else to go! Maybe he was safe for her in some way. Anyhow, people don't just up and leave in the middle of Montana when they've been driving with someone in a stolen car. Sometimes you just have to keep going, finish what you started. Sometimes it's the only thing to do."

"I would have gotten out, I most certainly would have."

"No you wouldn't—you'd hang on until the bitter end."

"Then you don't know me very well." That word of his jabs at her like a thorn. "Those guys in his stories just *cling* to some sorry Western myth they're a hundred years too late for." She feels a strange thrill at having said the word out loud and gotten away with it—his face didn't register a thing when she flung it at him across the room. Part of her wants to blow her cover now, confront him, but that would mean admitting to a greater crime.

She pours the hot water in the cup, takes a sip, makes a face. "Vile," she says.

He stands up. "Let's walk to that cafe we saw down the road. Road coffee beats motel coffee any day." He opens his briefcase, tucks his journal under his arm. "Are you going to bring yours?"

She stares at the brown leather cover. "No. I'll just read the paper."

They walk down the two-lane road along the bay. The water is listless and looks as if it's steaming, cooling from a rolling boil, though it's only mist and the water is surely cold.

The cafe is a half mile away. She can see the red neon coffee cup but can't make out the name. Some of their best conversations have taken place in cafes. The clatter of dishes and the country songs full of regret on the jukebox were conducive somehow to a kind of honesty and expansiveness they couldn't seem to conjure in more familiar rooms.

Not one car passes them the whole time they walk. A deer comes out of the woods tentatively at first, then boldly steps onto the road, pausing once at the curving double yellow line, then crosses to the other side and calmly bends its head to a thicket of flowers and blackberries along the shoulder. She's afraid for the deer so close to the road and worries that on their way back it will no longer be alive.

"Doesn't it see us?" she asks.

"If it does, it doesn't care."

The deer lifts its head and stares as they pass and she thinks that it witnesses rather than merely sees them. The first night they made love she stayed awake long afterward so she could watch him sleeping, to witness a part of him that he himself had never seen. He was more beautiful in that slack state, his body curled like a too-tall child in a small bed, tangled hopelessly in the covers. But suddenly he began to move his mouth as if he were trying to bite and tear something— she could hear his teeth gnashing, literally. He did not wake and it terrified her. What in the world was he dreaming about and why didn't he make a sound? It seemed that in some way he was not open to her, would never be open to her, that her voice, no matter what she said, could not reach or wake him.

❖ The cafe is empty. The ceiling fan stirs the haze of smoke rising from the pile of bacon that spatters on the black grill. She chooses two stools at the counter rather than a booth along the window and he smiles as a man in a mustard-stained apron slides two mugs in their direction. The coffee fills the thick chalk-white mugs, heavy as paperweights, traced with hairline fractures around the rim. He's always liked these mugs—calls them disappearing artifacts.

"Heaven," he says. He drinks half a cup, orders rye toast and juice.

"Same," she says to the man who looks as if he knew all along she'd say that even though she studied the hand-lettered menu over the grill for some time.

He gulps the rest of the coffee, and the man comes to fill it again.

"We're out of rye. Sorry."

"Wheat, then."

"You too?"

She nods. "No—make that an English muffin."

She wraps her hands around the mug. The word bites through again but she doesn't have a clue as to how to talk about it. Clinging. How can he say that about her? If anything, she thinks she's always been too much the opposite.

She remembers back a month ago to her grandfather's death, how surprised she was that she didn't cry until the day after the funeral when a hummingbird flew in through her open window and kept darting at the red pillow on the couch. How could it be that confused? Shouldn't instinct have told it something? That was when she cried, not so much for her grandfather at that moment, but for witnessing the sadness of a small mistake—or maybe on a hummingbird scale it was a colossal error—to love the color red so much you'd fly into a trap just to have it.

❖ The muffin comes, soaked in butter. She doesn't want to pick it up, let alone eat it. His toast looks drier, more appealing.

"Trade me?"

"Sure."

God, what an agreeable man. She wonders how he can gnash his teeth at night, how he can insult her in his journal and sit there smiling and give his toast away. And he's so *meticulous* about spreading the jam. She wants to grab the knife out of his hand and slam it, sticky, onto the counter.

She feels her anger building to critical mass and the habitual thickening of some internal wall to hold it back, but the first words leak through anyway, though they come out without particular inflection or volume. "Michael, I saw what you wrote."

He stops spreading jam. The knife is poised above the muffin and she watches a glob of liquefied strawberries gather at the tip, stretch downward toward the muffin and fall finally on the pitted surface. It takes forever.

"I was going to tell you." He puts down the knife and picks up his coffee, stares into the cup as if the bottom of that black liquid obscures the very words he's looking for.

"Tell me what—that you've been building up this resentment about me but just couldn't bring yourself to say what you really felt?"

"That it's over."

"Over? We haven't even talked about it yet."

"I'm not seeing her anymore."

Their bodies turn slowly on the counter stools toward each other. They stare.

"How much did you read?"

"Evidently not enough."

"Oh Christ." He turns away.

The cook comes at them. "Fresh pot," he calls out and pours them each a cup as if he's made it just for them. He has no idea of the damage he's walking into.

She braces herself against the counter as if she could push it away with her hands.

"How could you be so utterly stupid as to write it down?"

"Well you had no business—no business at all reading my journal!"

"So it serves me right, is that what you're saying?"

"I'm just saying you're overreacting. It was nothing—temporary insanity."

"What makes you think it's the temporary kind? Why shouldn't I think I'm temporary too?"

"Annie, I'm tired and I don't have any plans. I thought this weekend would help, and that's as far ahead as I can think right now."

"Then why did you open up to me?"

"It seemed right at the time."

"But not now."

"I don't know and I don't want to talk about it. I need some time to myself."

"That's what you said a month ago when you started hiking by yourself every Sunday—or was walking even on the agenda?"

She can't tell yet whether his lies are large or small or how far back they go. She tries to picture herself—doing what—standing in the kitchen making asparagus soup while he was out supposedly communing with nature but was really plunging himself deeper into some other woman's dreams. Or was she even at home—maybe she had been shopping, or drawing or reading, or something equally separate and oblivious.

Michael is trying to get the man's attention for the check. He turns to her and says, "I think we should take a break when we get back. Not see each other for a while."

She can't sit here any longer, can't drink that man's coffee, which is, after all, decent, can't eat the toast that seemed more appetizing than her own, can't even look at him anymore. She feels hot, needs to feel the complete cold of anger, something to constrict her back into her own shape again to counteract the welling up, the spilling over, the caving in and crying that so automatically happens when she's scared.

She gets up fast and knocks her glass over. The water pools onto the counter, then creeps toward the edge and spills in a long, thin waterfall to the floor.

"I thought you said I was somebody you could spend a long time with." She can see his handwriting on the journal page, how hopeful and fluid it seemed.

"I never said that." He pauses. "Did I?"

She pushes the screen door open and steps outside. The bay is as flat and gray as sheet metal. A single sailboat is stuck to the surface.

She hears the cash register ring, pictures Michael peeling money apart from the crumpled wad in his pocket. She turns around and without really planning to, leans her shoulder against the screen door, barricading it.

He pushes against it, and the door bows slightly at the top but does not open.

"Move away from the door, Annie."

She shakes her head. She will not be commanded like a child. She can't see him through the screen clearly, but he can see her, she's sure, even the small scar on her cheek that she's had so long she's forgotten where it came from although she remembers a fall, the odd sight of her blood on the grass. Michael used to explore the scar's slightly raised surface with the tip of his tongue as though he cherished both her survival and the calamity that had wounded her.

He pushes harder against the door and she throws her whole body against it as if by holding back the force behind it, a force like a wall of water, she can keep herself from harm.

"I'm going to kick it open if you don't move out of the way. What is the *matter* with you?"

He is right there on the other side of the screen, close enough to hear her if she whispered. There is no need to shout. The words enunciate themselves slowly, clearly.

"Fuck you, Michael. *Fuck* you."

She can't believe she said that—the word always sounded slightly trashy when she heard other people say it—a language of epithets heard late at night in convenience store parking lots, shouted from one drunk to another, not from her to a man she's wept and laughed and learned to sleep all the way through the night with. But it is, finally, the right word, and it seems thoroughly capable of inflicting a small wound he will always remember—the sound of that word coming from this woman who had saved it up all these years until it had true mass and velocity, hurled with the passion and conviction of a terrorist across a small, unwatched border.

❖ *Boojum*

Elaine waits beneath the *ramada,* only partially shaded from the relentless heat of late August in Loreto, Mexico. Her yellow canvas suitcase slouches next to her, and her sandals are a subdued pink, pale against the sun-dark color of her feet. She looks at her feet— the long toes, the high arches—and finds them not beautiful exactly, but, well... pretty. She lifts her head again. A halfhearted breeze disturbs the palm leaves in front of her. They rustle like cellophane and seem terribly shiny when the sun glances off them. She shifts from one foot to another and feels as thin as the slats that barely form a roof above her. She is exhausted as she waits though she has stood here for no more than ten minutes at most, and she lets her eyes travel slowly, wearily across the stretch of lawn in front of her— the only thing flourishing at the Mendez clinic. The gardener drags a dribbling hose from one tree to the next, a counterclockwise pattern of brief transfusions. He smokes a cigarette with great patience, the long exhalations briefly sketching the shape of his breath as he waits for the bowls of earth to fill.

She waits for Daniel, glad now she relented when he offered to meet her instead of taking a bus back home. She looks at her watch— ten after eight. He is barely late. Ten minutes is nothing, she tells herself, coming from such a distance, especially when it was arranged by letter, agreed to when she could not see his face at the end of the offer to know how to interpret it. "What are friends for?" he would have said face to face, but there was only handwritten script in which so much could be hidden. Eight-twelve. Maybe he changed his mind.

In the four weeks Elaine has spent here her sense of time has been drastically changed. The ritual of medication marked the clock. Laetrile was administered at specific intervals—one nurse in the morning when the slash of light from the window fell just to the left of the crucifix on the wall, another nurse in the evening when the shadow of the palm crossed her bed.

She is less than a month away from turning forty. Now that her body has gone awry, her house sold to pay the medical expenses, she feels, in all respects, without shelter. Roland's death two years before seemed more bearable in comparison. Before coming to Mexico, she rented a small efficiency apartment in Encino. She dreads the idea of going back there now, trying to cook in that cramped kitchen, she dreads no longer having a garden to sink her hands into.

Not sixth months after Roland died, she developed a cough that in a matter of weeks she could no longer ignore. The X rays betrayed her like surveillance photos—shadows in her lungs where shadows shouldn't be, blooming dark as black violets. After radiation, the new pictures showed new shadows grown from seed tufts that spread, blown by some internal wind.

She came to Mexico, changing the last of her savings to pesos at the border. Four weeks of injections and the inundation of the Spanish language. She became a small child again with a child's vocabulary of only the most necessary words: water, pain, please.

Dr. Mendez himself had come to her this morning, looked at her chart, and said, "*Señora, completo.*" And then in English, his most practiced and necessary phrase, "Now you must wait and see, no?"

The gardener coils the hose and turns off the tap. This takes a long time—he is as meticulous as a man laying fuse for dynamite. He will rest now, lean against a palm and smoke another cigarette, before he goes to the other end of the courtyard to the coiled hose there and begins the process all over again. This will take all morning. Waiting and seeing. So much easier to watch someone else.

Elaine shades her eyes and looking down the dirt drive sees the plume of dust coming half a mile away. A brown Dodge van with California plates, battered and dusty, the engine roaring through a hole in the muffler, churns up the gravel drive. A white dog hangs out the passenger window gulping down the breeze. The van rolls to a stop and is so covered with dust she can barely make out the words Daniel's Tree Service painted on the side. Daniel climbs out, waves his long arm in greeting. He is dressed in cut-offs and a T-shirt with a drawing of a hummingbird hovering over the approximate location of his heart. A silver oval belt buckle etched with a Hopi bear-paw print gleams from the center of his waist. A small earring glints in his left ear.

His beard has grown back since the last time she's seen him—he'd shaved it on a whim but seemed noticeably unprotected without it, and now the once-bare chin has been taken over again by a wild field the way weeds flourish in disturbed ground. Her very first impulse is to touch, but she takes the thought back quickly inside herself, as if it could, of its own volition, reach forward and brush his cheek without her full consent.

Daniel walks slowly toward her—all six-foot-three of him, angular and thin, and squints as she steps toward him into the full glare of the sun.

❖ It was parked at the end of her street one day. A brown van painted in yellow letters: FORMER FOREST RANGER in small capital letters, and beneath that in italics, *Palms a Specialty*. Roland was six months in the ground already, her illness only three months away.

Daniel was in a pine tree in the front yard of the house on the corner nearly hidden in the boughs, trimming branches with a small, almost delicate-looking saw.

"Hello," she called out, shading her eyes, leaning her head back as she looked up. "I have a dead tree in my yard—can you give me an estimate to cut it down?"

She pointed out her house and he promised to come by in an hour.

For the next three days Daniel took the eucalyptus apart, section by section. She watched him from behind the lacy veil of the dining room curtains. When he was done nothing remained except a depression in the earth where the stump had been. The dirt was soft there and he planted a bed of lobelia from seedlings.

Several days later she walked home with groceries to find the van parked in front of the house and Daniel in the backyard kneeling, planting a plum tree behind the lobelia.

"Reforestation," he said as he stood up. Brown patches of earth clung to his knees.

After that he came by regularly to bring her the odd plant he'd found and resurrected. He was quite the scavenger. "People just give up on plants at the first sign of aphids. You just have to wash them, that's all." She pictured him holding a dripping leaf, soaping its shiny surface, its paler underneath.

❖ He stands in the full sun before her now, damp crescents of sweat beneath his arms, the dark spots of his pupils next to nothing in the hazel-green eyes. How was she to know that this last month of near sensory deprivation would reveal him in such a vivid, unsettling way? She shifts her purse from one shoulder to the other. She can't for the life of her think what to say.

He speaks first. "You look good—rested."

She frowns. What a thing to say. A week ago she put the rings that would no longer stay on her fingers into a knotted handkerchief.

"No, really, Elaine."

"It's just the tan. I sat in the sun an hour a day."

"Well, it looks good on you." He squeezes her hand and that small act of tenderness nearly unhinges her. She retrieves her hand, unfolds the stems from a pair of sunglasses and pushes them quickly over her eyes, then fumbles to get them on straight. The English language, the fluency of simple sentences passing between them fills her with a sadness she hadn't counted on, a sharp contrast to the fragments of conversations with the other patients who spoke only in the monosyllabic pain of the body.

She had written him a single letter from the clinic and in it she had said, "What I miss most is working in the garden with you." She sat there for a long time, the ink drying, then added, "I think about you. Often." She supposes now it might have said more than she realized or was consciously prepared to express, or that he could have drawn something from it that was not intended. Just what was intended she is no longer sure of, but a few words brought him here and now she must think of something else to say.

She takes note again of the beard, which she now understands she's sorely missed, at the earring which her proper Bostonian upbringing would normally label as eccentric, if not flagrantly bizarre, and she is altogether relieved at his incongruity, at the diversion his very presence provides. She takes one of his hands into both of hers.

"I thought you'd never get here."

He bends to kiss her lightly on the forehead, a thing he's never done, and she feels the slight, not unpleasant abrasion of his mustache against her skin. She wonders how this looks. She turns her head to find the gardener but he's gone. In the next second it doesn't matter. She's too tired to consider her tangled feelings, to separate the strands of anticipation from those of fear and count which grow in greatest profusion.

He opens the door of the van. "Haywire, get in the back," and the dog jumps off the front seat into the rear of the van. Daniel swipes sand from the seat with his hand.

She turns her attention to the van. There's a jumbled pile of cassette tapes in the space between the seats—Vivaldi, Dire Straits, Satie—a dog dish near the gear shift, a deeply creased map of Baja with a stain of something sticky like honey or apricot jam over Ensenada. She turns in her seat, looks back at the dog who's curled on a mattress covered with a frayed but still beautiful patchwork quilt. A wooden milk crate filled with books— Chekhov, Rilke, Hillerman mysteries. A pair of binoculars swing from a hook. A camp stove, a cardboard box of food.

He clears his throat and says as she turns to look at him, "I thought you'd maybe like to take a trip, see some things as long as we're down here. You didn't sound like you were exactly looking forward to going home."

She doesn't quite know what to make of this but she's touched, his thinking of her, his planning something. And then her stomach tightens—this is the trip that people with limited time on earth take, a last sweep through the atmosphere, one last look at everything.

"What did you have in mind?" She leans her head back against the headrest.

"I thought we could drive down along the Sea of Cortez. I know you're short of money, but I've got enough food for a few days, and there's a mattress in back that you can sleep on. It's pretty comfortable."

She steals a glance at him. He is absolutely without guile.

"It's very sweet of you, but you don't have to do this, Daniel."

His voice rises to a defensive pitch. "I'm not trying to be *sweet*." The aftermath of the word hangs in the air like something sticky. He puts the key in the ignition but doesn't turn it.

"I just want to spend some time with you before we go back to all that." He gestures north, toward the United States.

"Some vacation—driving around Baja with a forty-five-year-old woman on her last legs."

He leans back, his fingers grip the steering wheel. He's looking straight ahead, then closes his eyes when he says, "Jesus,

Elaine—don't talk like that about yourself. Don't even fucking *think* it."

Then he looks at her. "Besides. I'm thirty, remember? Not exactly a different generation. And I've got a child of my own." He pauses. "Had," he says. He fiddles with the keys, pumps the gas pedal hard, starts the engine, which falters, slams the pedal once more until it catches.

"What if I say yes?" She looks straight ahead when she says it and realizes that it sounds like a threat.

He looks out the window as a white-robed sister glides across the lawn balancing a tray of clinking vials. "Then we get the hell away from here—we just start driving."

She watches the Mexican gardener cross the courtyard. He sees her watching him and moves his arm in a gesture that is half wave, half salute. Just driving away is Daniel's style, but right now it seems appealingly reckless.

"All right," she says.

His face, which seemed tense a moment ago, ready for refusal, relaxes. He picks up the map, unfolds it quickly before she can change her mind, and points to a city on the Sea of Cortez. "We could make it to La Paz by tonight. I'll drive slow. Promise."

Good. She no longer wants to get anywhere in a hurry.

❖   The seat of the van is hot to the touch and she can feel the backs of her thighs slowly adhere, the curve of her spine conform to the shape of the bucket seat with each passing kilometer. She has the sensation of falling south, as if the continent were slowly upended and everything sent sliding toward the sun. The shapes of cactus seem fantastic—green claws reaching out of the baked ground. "Organ pipe," Daniel says. "If they made music it would only be Bach fugues, bass notes to shake your sternum."

Elaine smiles, her lips dry, sealed together. Such a change to be driven. All her married life she'd been the sole driver, arranging Roland's itineraries. Bach fugues. Roland never did anything but sing beautifully. Elaine had been his accompanist in the rehearsals at the Providence opera company—a small, underpaid, dedicated group. When the first (and last) season closed, she and Roland got married, then went to Pasadena to join another company. As Roland's wife and twenty years his junior, she was still his accompanist, though she no longer played. She made all the nonmusical arrangements. She was more road manager than wife, and for years they lived in hotels when the company went on tour, once even to Portugal and Spain. Pasadena was a resting place between journeys. Opera had its own rhythm, its particular seasons, a rhythm Elaine was accustomed to. She knew the cities, the halls, the small entourage of fans who greeted them year after year. While Roland rehearsed, Elaine wandered the botanical gardens and planetariums, reveling in the things she could see and touch rather than hear. And then everything changed all at once—Roland dying in a restaurant, of all places, lurching forward without a sound, then crumpling in the corner of the red leather booth. Aneurism. No lingering pain, no hospital visits, no exposure in one's pajamas to strangers. Roland made an exit, intact. And he left nothing behind—no life insurance (it never occurred to him), a modest savings, just the equity in the house they'd hardly ever lived in. So after years of living on Roland's terms, the sex that was more afterthought than desire, the half-life of hotel rooms, their comings and goings subject to the whims of agents and audiences, she returned to the house in Pasadena and moved in for the first time. The inside of the house was of much less interest to her than the outside and she spent most of her time in the garden, making a conscious effort at some kind of order, planning it so that in any given month she could look forward to something coming into flower.

She was working on a patch of aromatic herbs that Daniel had helped to plant when she was diagnosed with cancer. Without insurance she had no choice but to sell the house. The realtor was delighted with the garden. "An enhancement—street appeal," he said. As though she'd worked that earth and stooped in the sun to attract a buyer, as though she'd ever thought someone else would ever have it.

Daniel disappeared for about a week right around that time, and Elaine couldn't help but feel that he was pulling away from the increasing weight of her losses. She didn't really blame him, but still she felt betrayed.

The night before she moved out she stood alone on the front porch in the dark. The lilacs looked almost white in the moonlight, heavy with its own profusion. She took a pair of scissors and, one by one, she snipped the lilacs, tossing them on the porch. The scent was overpowering and she'd never felt anything softer when the soles of her bare feet pressed them into the floor.

❖ It's the absence of noise that starts to wake her, the lull after the steady whine of the engine laboring around the endless turns. Daniel's hand is on her arm, his voice travels toward her in the dark.

"You must have needed that sleep—you didn't blink an eye when that truck nearly forced me off the road a while back."

She smiles, pleased that her body felt safe enough to sleep.

"I'll help you out—you should see this."

He stands by the open door. She braces her hand against his shoulder to climb down. She feels stiff from the long ride, and terribly weak as she brings her feet to earth. Below, the city of La Paz lies tucked in a curved arm of land. Lights mark the waterline, and the moon— nearly full—casts a metallic blue sheen on the bay. An island, unmarked by lights, lies offshore, a great hulking shape in the night.

Elaine feels a twist of pain in her chest, closes her eyes until it passes, opens them onto the same scene: lights on the water, the moon lifting into the night.

Haywire, who jumped out of the van ahead of her, is out there zigzagging, nose to the ground, peeing every so often on a bush. He comes back eventually to where they stand and sits quietly beside them, pushing his head beneath her hand.

"There's a beach down there where we can make camp."

He's only thought it out this far—taking her to La Paz, the journey that took all day during which he had nothing to do but drive and she to look out the window or sleep. She's hardly been anywhere with him outside of the garden, never had to confer on anything besides the best kind of fertilizer for evergreens or the right amount of space between planting beds. She doesn't know his deeper preferences or idiosyncrasies, nor he hers. Maybe he's not good at anything but gardening—maybe that's why he lives alone. What was she thinking of in agreeing to this? The idea of countless inconsequential negotiations suddenly seems daunting to her.

She leaves the decision to him. "Whatever you think." She's not helping any, she knows. But she wants at this point simply to be passive, to be taken somewhere, for food to be put in her hand, for a blanket to be draped around her. She'd fought against her illness and what good did it do her? Let someone else do battle now.

They climb back into the van and head out of the mountains and high plateaus, down into the fields, the flat stretch of land that leads to water. On the edge of town Daniel turns down an unpaved street past brightly lit houses. Dogs that had been sleeping in the road blink in the headlights and stagger to the side as they drive past. The van comes to a stop on a sandy beach near a small cantina. She can hear music drifting toward them from an outdoor patio, occasional laughter.

They sit on a blanket in the sand eating tortillas and beans, roasted green chiles. He's forgotten napkins. She sucks her fingers, then wipes them on her dress. The bottled water is warm, the cups a little sandy. As the moon climbs overhead, the light on the water widens.

❖ She remembers the transition they made from the garden to the kitchen when she still had the house. She had him over to breakfast. The room was filled with sunlight and the shadows of oleander leaves from outside the window. He said that he used to be a park ranger in Palomar State Park, that he made friends with the night watchman at the observatory and spent hours looking through the telescope at the reddish gaseous clouds of nebulae. She was delighted with this and took him downstairs to the den to show him the glow-in-the-dark stars she had meticulously pasted on the ceiling, following a map of the constellations. She switched the light off and the stars flashed on all at once. She pointed out the Pleiades, Ursa Major, Pegasus, but she couldn't quite see her hand. He was quiet for a time, just looking up, then he began to tell her about his divorce from his wife and his four-year-old daughter two years earlier, his letters to them returned to sender. He quit his job as an untenured English teacher at the university, packed up his belongings, and headed east to the Sierra. He took temporary jobs, spent a summer staring at the tops of trees watching for the first sign of smoke to curl above them. She talked of Barcelona and Lisbon, fado singers in dim cafes, streets of vendors selling birds and flowers, until the stars on the ceiling faded, their brief, stored-up light leaking away.

❖ Now she sits on this Mexican beach not two feet from the man she first saw in a tree. He pours coffee into two mugs as if he's done it all their lives. She buries her feet in the sand, then wiggles her toes free. Now there isn't so much a future as a sense of open space in front of her, in which to do anything she damn well pleases. But what does she please? She feels heavy, like a bent figure dragging two suitcases through a huge terminal toward a distant gate, without a clue as to being anything other than the Elaine she's always been.

She looks at Daniel stirring sugar in her coffee. She tries to imagine herself naked with this man but she can't. Whatever pleasure her body was capable of has atrophied. It seems a strain to lift the coffee, bring it to her lips. Sip. Swallow. She has to command each motion and gesture. Nothing is natural. She's not willing to try to arouse herself and to fail at it. She prefers to think of her energy and desire as latent—there to be summoned if she wants—and she can think this way as long as she doesn't actually move.

Daniel looks at the water. Elaine likes how his hands curve around the cup, his long, slender feet, the high arches, the arteries climbing his calves, the bony islands of his knees. But his face is unreadable. For all his solid physicality she feels a guarded distance there too, as if he shows only the parts of himself that can be of specific use.

He points to a group of stars rising above the water. "Cassiopeia, right?"

She nods. She's pleased to have given something back, to be someone associated with stars.

He rolls out his sleeping bag on the sand and she climbs into her bed in the van. She leaves the side door open. The fire he built an hour ago has burned down. She can almost see his face in the last of its light.

"Peso for your thoughts."

He sighs. She can feel him struggling with words.

"Sometimes I'm glad you don't seem to need anything from me. Sometimes I wish you did."

"I don't know how to need anything anymore. Counting on anyone seems desperately unfair."

"It's all unfair. People always need more than they can say or less than they can admit to." He turns in his sleeping bag to lie face up. "My family, my ex-family, needed something."

She's not sure she wants to hear this. "Look, you don't have to tell me—"

"But that's just it. I do have to."

"Why? Why now?"

"Because it's Mexico. Because it's Tuesday. Because you of all people might understand."

She can feel it coming, the backlash of his other life, the one he's only alluded to before, the one that will change the way she knows him, and for the first time she understands the man in *Last Tango in Paris,* why he forbade his lover to tell him her name.

"The last time I saw my daughter, Carrie, she was three, and Sarah and I had just found out that she was autistic and would never be what the doctors call functional. Functional—sounds more like furniture than a person. Sarah made the decision—I couldn't—to put her in a state school. But I didn't fight her on it either."

He pauses for a second. "Should I stop?" He doesn't wait for an answer, but keeps right on.

"I always knew that something wasn't right, but I kept thinking she's just a baby, she's just taking her time to grow. But Jesus, I'd go to pick her up and she'd just pull away, or throw a fit. If she hurt herself she wouldn't cry and I never had the faintest idea if she felt happy, ever, or if I could even make her sad. Then Sarah and I started acting like that around each other. I knew sometimes when we looked at each other we both were thinking things we couldn't possibly say—'This has to be *your* fault.' Having a child in the first place began to feel like a mistake. The day Sarah took Carrie to the state school I said at the last minute I just couldn't go. Sarah didn't argue with me or even try to talk. Carrie was just sitting there, strapped in her car seat looking straight ahead at nothing. I tapped on the window and when she turned her head to the noise, I waved. She didn't wave back—she never did—she just looked at me like I was anybody, like I had nothing to do with her. Sarah stalled the VW and couldn't get it started again. That always happened with that goddamn car—you'd think it could have made a concession that day. So I ran behind the car and pushed them down the street. Sarah was taking forever to pop the clutch so I banged my fist on the roof. The car jerked and almost stopped, then the engine caught. And then she just drove away.

"I stood in the middle of the street a long time. I looked at the rows of bungalows, the flowers and hedges and bikes in driveways, and when I looked at my own house it didn't look like my home, but like some place where I used to live. So I left. I left even before Sarah got back. I couldn't imagine having a conversation with her, or cooking dinner, or even sleeping in the same bed."

He stops. The silence is more frightening than his story. None of this particularly surprises her and she sees his stripped-down life as an effort at atonement, both futile and alluringly possible. She would like to tell him about the fear that keeps her breathing shallow, the fear that inches along her spine. An exchange of secrets. She learned long ago that there are certain advantages to keeping still, and though that habit doesn't feel useful anymore, it's too ingrained to alter. The other reason she can't tell him about her fear is that he's a contributor, a long shot when she wants predictable odds. A sudden pain twists in her side. She pictures a frayed rope stretched taut, the braids springing loose one at a time.

"Daniel—I don't want to be someone you experiment on until you get it right."

He doesn't answer. She hears only faint music drifting from the cantina, a guitar, a voice, the unmistakable roll and turn of Spanish syllables like the current of a deep river. She waited too long to say it. Daniel's breathing has already deepened into the mindless rhythm of sleep, or else he's run out of things to confess.

Her fingers press against her ribs, tracing them like the slats of a fence, teeth of a wide-toothed comb. She fingers the ridge of a scar that plunges straight from navel to pubis. The things that have been going on inside her seem mutinous, and she finds herself going back over the years trying to understand if she'd given her body due cause, shorted it somehow in what it most wanted so that it stole from her. She remembered coming back from the Austrian tour after Roland's funeral, walking up the steps to her house. It looked like her house from the outside, but inside it was stripped of its treasures, the skin of its back windows ruptured and all the things that had given her comfort carried away. Thieves she could almost understand in their simple greed, but the idea of a thief loose in her body terrifies her— she can't drive it out or just pack up and leave. Maybe Daniel could, but she can't.

After she sold the house, and he came back from wherever he had disappeared to for that week—he didn't volunteer any information and she didn't feel she had the right to ask—he helped her move to the small apartment in Encino. He was there when she wrapped the scarf around her bare head, still there six months later when she took it off again. Her hair had grown back gray, brushy, and surprisingly soft like the first crew cut on a boy.

"You look like Grace Jones."

"Who's that?"

"A woman who sings. A rock singer. All you need is black leather and a white guitar."

She laughed. "I'd wake the dead." She pictured Roland covering his ears.

❖ She peels back the quilt which now feels uncomfortably heavy on her skin. She wants to walk, something the clinic never allowed at night. She pulls on a pair of sweatpants and slips out of the van.

The sand is cool, the lights of the cantina shimmer behind the courtyard palms as she comes nearer. Haywire saunters up to her and she peers in the dark behind her for Daniel, but he isn't there. Another dog, a white mongrel, walks stiffly toward them from the right, touches noses with Haywire in a friendly, tired way, then flops down in the sand.

Music drifts over the patio wall. The singer's voice cracks on the high notes. Roland would be appalled. She moves toward the steps leading to the patio to see if she can catch a glimpse of the singer. Couples move together in slow circles beneath a blue, smoky haze. A white skirt flares in the breeze. A dark hand encircles a waist. Lamps waver on the rippled surface of a fountain pool. The stray dog trots in a rather lopsided gait down the beach until it, too, is a white shape moving in the dark.

❖ The embers of the fire breathe slightly in the breeze, glowing like collapsing stars. Daniel's sleeping bag is flat, a shed skin. She pats it absurdly. But clearly he's gone and she feels engulfed in a sickening dread, not so much at the idea of being alone, but that he mattered so much, so soon.

She walks down the beach, tries to call to him but can find no more than a hoarse whisper. Exhausted, she sinks to the sand. She tries to stand again but cannot. It's too dizzy up there and her slender frame tilts, as if in a gale. Something in her longs right now for the ground. So she crawls back the way she came, covering the distance of a hundred yards in the determined way of small children who are capable of walking but won't.

She reaches the sleeping bag and it seems like a raft she climbs onto. She doesn't hear him come up beside her, but feels his hand on her shoulder, the sensation of heat seeping into her skin.

"Where were you? I've been up and down the beach looking."

She turns to him. The moon has set. She can hardly see his face in the dark. "Everything scares the hell out of me now. Even you."

He sits down next to her, gets her to sit in front of him. His hands massage her shoulders. His legs stretch out on either side of her, long as oars.

Her tears are hot and silent. He leans forward. She can feel his penis harden against the small of her back and when he pulls away slightly as if in apology, she leans back and pulls him closer. More surprising than the solid feel of his chest breathing into her back is the way he draws her knees up, the way his hands hold her bare feet so that she has the feeling of being completely held, all the separate things in her that were flying apart, gathered.

❖ She wakes in the same position she was in when she had fallen asleep—on her left side, curved into the template of his body.

Daniel slips from beneath the blanket. He fiddles with the Coleman stove, coaxing a blue flame from it to heat water for coffee. Elaine sits up. He stops what he's doing for a second. No averted glances, just the intimacy that does not come from specific sex but from the gestures closest to it.

He flips the tortillas over and the edges curl and darken with heat.

Everything seems ordinary and reassuring. They savor the coffee, look often at the water, one or the other of them pointing out a pelican's spectacular, reckless dive, the far-off plume of spray from a sounding whale.

After breakfast they walk down the beach. They walk past white walls with bougainvillea flung over the top and dripping down the side like a crimson spray. Her hair warms in the sun and grows fragrant with heat. The pores of her skin open. Daniel stoops often to scoop up flat stones, his arms flinging them back into the sea. For all his arm-swinging, they land not far away, and none of them skip the way he wants them to.

He stops in the shade of an old decaying palm by the broken brickwork of a once-tended courtyard. He points. "It's a boojum," he says, as if unveiling it.

"A what?"

"A boojum—it's a tree."

She's expecting to look up, to see something towering beyond the palm, but it's short for a tree, the size of a tall person, the shape of an upside-down parsnip, the texture of an elephant's knee.

She moves forward for a closer look. Thin stems notched in simple leaves grow upward like a sweet potato sprouting in a jar.

"This one's out of its habitat. There's a forest of them up the coast—some fifty feet tall that loop back on themselves as if they can't quite make up their minds which direction they want to grow in. We can go see them tomorrow if you want."

She likes that he knows where this tree comes from—a wanderer from a small, close-knit clan. She watches, in mild surprise, how her hand so casually, with such ease and familiarity, slides into the back pocket of his jeans, how as soon as he feels her hand there he turns to face her.

With the other hand she points, and he turns his head to follow what she shows him—just above the boojum's arid leaves, its one gesture of extravagance. The yellow flag. The flowers.

❖ *Azimuth*

What Sam remembers is the act of falling, not the impact itself, a sense of flight rather than the memory of the ground rushing up to meet him. Even after he fell from the horse, he stayed in midair, hovering between one world and another. He heard a word sneak under the blanket of darkness—"coma"—but he thought of his condition as one of acute ambivalence. He couldn't decide whether to stay or to leave. He listened with half an ear to the nearly familiar voice of a woman who stood by the bed and all the tones she tried over that two-week time—cajoling, scolding, pleading. She had tried everything to bring him back. When he thought about it, he believed he loved the woman who leaned over him, but he couldn't remember how he first met her, or what it was about her that drew him to her. The limbo of the coma gave him a choice. He could leave her, not for someone else, really, but for a weightless, guilt-free world. A world that could allow him to go soft and sleepy, where he would not always have to be hard and ready. A world where he could be inarticulate and forgiven.

He is vaguely aware of the machinery that keeps track of him,
gauges that sense when he slips farther away, but the best part, he
thinks, of being unconscious and out of range is that he can be as
unpredictable as a child even though he must be—what, fifty or sixty
years old? And he is a child. If he turns his head or opens one eye
even halfway it is cause for celebration—the nurses write it down.
He senses *her* there, flexes the fingers of the hand she holds. Is it the
right, or the left? He hears her gasp. That small gesture—to her it's
nothing short of miraculous.

❖ Hannah is asleep by the bed in a straight-backed chair. Sam's hand
moves under her grasp. When she opens her eyes his eyes are open
too, blue as always, but looking at her from an enormous distance.

"Sam . . . " She's at a complete loss for other words. Already she's
begun to think of him in the past tense.

She met him fifteen years ago, the day after her thirtieth birthday
on her first trip to Arizona—a group tour from Oxford making the
rounds of the archaeological sites of the Southwest. The last stop on
the trip had been Tucson, for the annual rodeo. She'd left her fellow
professors sitting on the bleachers shielding their Anglo-Saxon skin
from the vertical sunlight with the mainstay of their own country—
black umbrellas—dour and funereal in the bright arena. She wandered the long row of stalls where the horses were fed and groomed
and readied for their events. Sam was bent over a silver saddle, pol-
ishing it with a chamois cloth. She'd never seen a saddle like it and
stopped to get a closer look.

"The only silver I've ever polished is my grandmother's tea
service."

He looked up, and she felt startled even though he smiled. If she
could have picked an image of the American Cowboy he would have
been it: six-foot-three, angular and lean, but strong, sun-dark skin
lined with the imprints of a bright, hot climate. He had a combina-
tion of verbal shyness and physical strength, which she found terribly attractive.

Finally, he said, "You sound like you're from somewhere else."

"England."

"Oh."

"I've never seen a saddle like this. I've only ridden English saddle—flat and plain as a platter compared to this." She touched the silver, the tooled leather.

"Want to try it out?" He smiled again but, as soon as she smiled back, looked down at her hands tracing the leather roses on the saddle.

"That would be lovely."

He saddled the gelding quarter horse, carefully tightened the girth, shortened the leather stirrups for her. She moved close to the horse to mount, hesitated, waiting for him to give her a leg up, imagining how her knee would feel cupped briefly in his hands, how her body would feel being lifted by him to settle into a saddle as ornate as a throne. He made no move to help her.

She lifted herself up, looked down at him holding the reins. She held out her hand for them. He hesitated.

"I know how to ride."

He turned over the reins he'd just spent an hour saddle-soaping. She pulled on the left rein to turn the horse around but he just stamped his foot and didn't move.

"He doesn't understand that way—you have to lay the reins across his neck from the right to turn him left—that's what he knows."

The horse responded immediately.

He was glad he had something to tell her she didn't already know.

She rode a short distance and came back to the stall, swung her long leg over the horse to step down to the ground again. She thanked him.

"You like Mexican food?"

"Well I've never had the pleasure."

"I know a good place."

"Are you extending an invitation?"

"Guess I am."

❖ They fell in love fast, both of them feeling lucky for different reasons. They were somewhat exotic to each other, but their common ground was horses, and land to ride them on.

She adapted quickly to the desert, loved the insistent, dry heat on her skin that was so tired of dampness. Loved the ubiquitous saguaro cactus in their similar but never-the-same shapes, the raw, unfinished edges of the mountains in any direction she looked, the vast expanse of sky that seemed more like the ocean than the North Sea did. Loved the man next to her she'd seen the likes of only in films, his stubborn quietness, his passionate, almost primitive abandon in bed, his physical strength he took so much for granted, his love of his land. She wrote long, descriptive letters home to friends, who thought her decision to marry him impetuous and told her that she would undoubtedly return to her native home in due time. She surprised them all by staying on. She didn't miss the scholarly, cloistered existence. She felt she had graduated to a simpler, more physical life. If she'd still been at Oxford and read about a woman in her position she would have envied her.

❖ Hannah leans forward, gripping his hand. Sam's mouth opens, then closes, then opens again, like a fish stunned by the air after it's caught. His eyes narrow with the effort of concentration and he turns his head from side to side like a furious child in the midst of a tantrum. He lifts his hand up, still clutched tightly around hers, then brings them both down hard on the bed over and over again.

❖ Sam was convinced after the first year with Hannah that he would one day run out of things to teach her. She seemed to have a hunger for learning anything new and he wondered how long he could hold her. In the evenings she read and there were books on every table and nightstand, towering under the reading lamps. He had barely finished high school, had to stay an extra summer taking history and literature over again just to graduate. He was working then on his father's ranch, which would be left to him in just a few years. The place took nearly all of his time. He couldn't imagine all those words streaming inside her, how they all fit, how they made her excited or sad, how they could move or change her.

❖ The ambivalence shifts ever so slightly, enough to let him fully wake. But what he hasn't counted on is leaving part of himself behind. Aphasia, the doctors call it. A graceful name, like a goddess's. Waking is only half the battle.

Another week and they pronounce him ready to go home. Where is that exactly? When she turns the pickup into the long gravel drive the saguaros seem both alien and familiar shapes to him, the way a garden hose, for instance, looks to a cat that has never seen a snake but carries a picture of the shape in its mind.

"Well, here we are," she says proudly as she shuts off the engine.

What an odd thing for her to say. She assumes so much, as though love were indelible, that all it takes is to see what you once loved and the feelings will come flooding back again.

❖ Hannah can walk this path blindfolded. She knows each dip and turn, the precise degree to which she must bend to clear the branch of mesquite that overhangs the arroyo. Today it catches her, holds her crouched beneath the limb until she can reach up, find the curved thorn and pull it from the back of her shirt. As careful as she is, the cloth tears.

She makes it the rest of the way to the picture rocks unimpeded but finds herself climbing to her familiar vantage point in a hurry as if the low outcropping is safer than the desert below. Before her, Safford Peak rears up from the Tucson Mountains, the end of the range.

For a moment she's distracted from the long view and her gaze drops to one of the granite rocks just below her, a rock scratched with petroglyphs, messages from the lost tribe of the Hohokam whose language was never written down. No one left alive speaks it anymore. The shape of one of the petroglyphs is distinctly that of a deer, his rack of horns tilted toward the ground where he grazes. A spiral sun rises behind him. What would she draw, if she had to, if words failed her the way they are still failing Sam, untold conversations stranded in his mind?

His first day home he had gone straight to the barn and she left him alone until dinner. She set their places on the table beneath the *ramada,* served his favorite meal: chicken *mole.* But when he sat down he just stared at it sullenly, picked at it as if he'd never seen it before.

"It's your favorite," she reminded him.

"Is it?" he said, looking genuinely confused.

The doctors had told her this sometimes happened—that people coming out of comas no longer liked what they'd always enjoyed before. Somewhere in that darkness their preferences changed. Did the change extend also to love, or was that etched in a deeper, different part of the brain?

❖ Hannah takes a sharp stone from the rubble at her feet. She begins to scratch on a boulder's rough surface the stick figure of a woman, hands raised above her head, fingers spread, like she's reaching for something solid in the air, or a gun is pointed toward her. Surrender or salutation, she isn't sure.

Sam is back where the path begins, home but not home, tending the horses, listening to the music drifting from the radio in the barn as he stacks hay. She can barely make him out from here. He's an indistinct shape moving in the corral, an outline of a man in a hat, bending in the heat.

❖ The coarse hair of the mare's tail feels as thick as twine in his hands. Was it always like this? He looks at it, combs his fingers through the tangle. Everything feels different. Even the sun is like a hand pressing down every last one of a hundred and ten degrees into the top of his head.

He keeps a yellow pad of paper in the barn to keep track of how much grain they use. These days he keeps it hidden beneath a pile of saddle blankets in the tack room. When Hannah isn't around he takes the pad out and writes between the columns as if those tiered numbers could protect the fragments of sentences like sheltering trees. Today he writes:

She wore yellow, so I liked her.
She said silver—so it shines.
Fiesta de los Vaqueros.
February?
This is mine. Don't look.
Posted: No Trespassing. Keep Out!

He feels Hannah coming down the path before he actually sees her, as if her tall form could throw a quarter-mile shadow. Has he always liked tall women? He can't remember. He wishes she were shorter, that her head came no higher than his heart. He puts the pad of paper away.

Sam unloads hay from the pickup. His shirt hangs from a post, limp as a flag on a windless day. Hannah stands and watches the muscles work in his back, remembering the feel of those muscles beneath her hands, the way he used to move above her, with her. The first night they tried to make love after he came home from the hospital he lost his erection as soon as he entered her. That had never happened before. "It's all right," she said, stroking his back. But it wasn't all right, not to him, and he wished she hadn't said anything.

These days he lies silent in bed, unable or unwilling to try the last kind of speech they might still be fluent in. But out here, in the barn where he doesn't have to speak or remember, where the animals notice no change in him, he now spends most of his time.

She has the odd sensation of fading like a once bright color left too long in the sun. He used to say he loved the sound of her name. He said it out loud, often. Now she wonders if he even remembers it.

A thought breaks through and it comes to her, standing in the shadow of the barn, watching this stranger work, that he is not a man she would have married.

❖ He turns toward her, squinting at her shape as she steps into the sunlight. "Did you feed . . . " he begins, looks toward the nearest stall at the foal who pokes his head over the half-door. Sam's face contorts with concentration as he gropes in a dark pool of countless words and names for the right one, the only one. Hannah struggles to keep from saying "Yazzie," to avoid, as his doctors have advised, completing his sentences for him. They stand there with the half-finished sentence ricocheting off the walls. She can't look directly at him anymore. She turns to the foal, takes a fistful of its mane and combs it out. She braids a strand but has nothing to tie it off with; it will soon come undone.

Sam paces wildly. "Shit," he yells. "Shit," he yells again, louder. Other words dam up inside his head but only the curses come through. He kicks the sheet-metal door and the whole building booms like thunder. He kicks it again, harder. The other two horses rear in their stalls and lash out with their hind hooves. The vibrations build to a deafening roar. Sam holds his hands to his ears and doubles over in a crouch as if shielding himself from a blow. These days even the slightest noise at the wrong time can unhinge him.

Hannah grabs the lead line attached to the foal's halter and unsnaps it from the ring riveted to the stall door. The foal dances on his delicate hooves, whirling, eyes rolled back. Her eyes move quickly from the horse to Sam, her attention split between their separate but related terrors. She lets go of the foal so he can escape the noise and he bolts out the door into the glaring sunlight, which seems to stop him like a deer in the blade of a high beam. He stiffens his legs, braking in the churning dust near the corral. He drops his head, shuddering, dust rising around him like a cloud.

She turns back to Sam. The air still feels shredded with his rage.

"What is it? What's the matter?" She looks at him, helpless with her own frustration, and he's giving her no clues. She says, "I don't know how to act. I don't think I even know you anymore."

Sam seems visibly struck by her words. In the old days he would have fired back a few of his own, and Hannah wishes for an argument, to connect in anger if in nothing else. But he just turns, throws the metal comb he's been holding all this time onto the ground, and stalks out of the barn.

❖ The land across the road is for sale now, their longtime neighbors succumbing to long-term illnesses, needing cash to sustain intensive care. A lifetime of land and the animals that grazed it, sold off to buy a little time. The chances of a private owner buying that ranch are slim—land is too expensive to simply dwell on anymore. Developers are already making their bids and the public hearing on the proposed zoning ordinance seems a futile gesture, but Sam and Hannah go, as they've always gone to these meetings, looking for some small loophole to prevent yet another deal from going down.

This afternoon, this last buffer zone between their land and Saguaro National Monument is up for grabs. The developers have a plan to build a "family community," carve the desert into "ranchettes" and convenience store lots, all of which mean the inevitable raising of taxes.

Sam and Hannah arrive late, sit down just in time to hear a council member propose high-density housing on the old Cortaro ranch property. Sam stands up to speak and stops, flailing for some word just beyond his reach, and he just stands there, mouth open, face reddening with shame at his failure to begin a simple sentence. His eyes fill with tears and Hannah takes his hand. She should have known he was not ready for this.

She stands up too, and says what she knows he would have said—"It's unmitigated greed! You used to be our neighbors and friends before the developers got to you with holidays in Hawaii and brand-new cars." She hears whispers, murmurs, but nobody says a word out loud.

Sam pulls her to the door away from the stares of their neighbors. He holds the keys as if he doesn't know what they belong to and she takes them from him, drives him home. Like a drunk, a voice inside her jeers, and she is immediately ashamed of herself for even thinking it.

Ten miles and not a word. The sun is long gone but light limns the edges of dark mountains, suffusing the sky closest to earth with a saffron glow. The near dark is safe somehow, but each time a car comes toward them, leaving its brights on a little too long, she can see him out of the corner of her eye, his strength ebbing by degrees.

"Ruined it," he said.

Tucson is growing a new mile north every year. The ranch, once well outside, is close to being crowded. One look at the lights at night shows it graphically, indisputably—they are in the thick of it.

When she parks the truck at the house, he swings himself out and stands there, staring up at the moon that's just coming up over the Rincons. She walks over to him, puts her arms around him from behind.

He can feel her breath on the back of his neck.

She begins to run her hands down his shoulders.

"Stop it."

She freezes, slowly drops her arms to her sides, pulls her mouth away from his earlobe. She had wanted to reach the tip of her tongue inside his ear, reach inside, make him hear.

He puts his hand over his ear as if she's said something wicked.

He takes the keys from her, then gets back in the truck, slamming the door once on the seatbelt. He pulls it out of the way, then yanks the door closed.

"Don't," she begins, but stops, reduced to single-syllable words when whole paragraphs are clamoring in her head.

"Be back percolator."

"*What?*"

He bangs his fist on the steering wheel. "Later, later later." He bangs the steering wheel again and the horn blares back at him. He can think the right words in his mind but sometimes the wrong words come out. He pictures himself a vending machine, the circuitry shorted, gone awry.

❖ First there's the rattle of the fenders as Sam crosses the cattle guard, then the flag of dust unfurling behind him. Next the tires' hum on the asphalt, the gears shifting, the engine's fading whine. Then nothing. It takes her a minute to realize she's shaking hard.

In a daze, she walks back to the house. She takes off her boots, strips away the damp sheath of her clothes, and lies back on the double bed. She looks up at the ceiling fan and she can almost feel the blades of shadow beating across her body.

She thinks about getting up to shower, thinks about not getting up, of letting Sam find her like this when he returns, confronting him with her nakedness. Her nipples harden despite the heat. And then she touches herself, something she hasn't done since she was a girl. She yields to her own hand, an act of which she is nearly ashamed, as if it signifies defeat. She tries to imagine Sam watching her, tries to imagine how he would see her—sensuous or ridiculous? She honestly couldn't say.

For all their trying, they never were able to have a child. The land became the thing they felt joy or worry for. In the days before the big resorts were built in the foothills, they'd had paying guests at the ranch, but before long they couldn't compete with tennis courts, swimming pools, color brochures. She remembers vividly when Sam sold twenty acres for taxes a year ago and didn't tell her until the deal was done. The surveyors came, severing that stretch of desert from them with something no thicker than fishing line. The day the bulldozers arrived, neither she nor Sam could bear the sound, nor could they talk to each other. In a matter of weeks the desert they'd carefully traced with riding trails threading through cactus and mesquite would be scraped clean by bulldozers, the cactus shipped

off on trucks to be sold in nurseries, or, even worse, brought back
to plant beside concrete driveways where they would survive less
than a year. They couldn't watch the surveyors carve it up like a piece
of meat. They got in the truck and drove all afternoon, ending up
at the Chiricahua Apache memorial near Portal, wanting to find the
crude pile of stones that marked the formal surrender of land to the
government before the entire tribe was shipped off, including Geron-
imo, in cattle cars to Florida.

The two of them stood, knee deep in the sweet grass, awkward
in their first grief together. Hannah took a black stone from her
jacket pocket, a stone worn smooth from rubbing her thumb across
it whenever she walked. A worry stone, Sam had called it when he
gave it to her.

She added it to the pile of rocks before her and it slipped into a
space between the larger, rougher ones. Sam pulled her close. She
felt the worn flannel of his shirt, the pressure of a pearl button
against her chin, and when she pulled away minutes later, her skin
was imprinted with its crescent. He told her it looked like a new
moon, that it must be a good sign of something. That night they made
love like two people who'd lost a child, so careful with each other,
as if any sudden movement would break them open. She wonders
now, lying on this same bed, if they can ever again be that tender
with each other.

❖ Sam's headlights sweep across the Land for Sale sign as he turns
onto Silverbell Road. Wind swirls the sand into dust devils—there's
no vegetation left to hold it down. In the beam of light that reaches
down the newly widened road he sees a tawny-colored animal running along the shoulder. At first he thinks it's a coyote, but because
it doesn't veer for cover, because he sees the uncertainty in its tail-
tucked stride, he knows it is a dog. He's close enough now to see it's
a female, that she is lost and trying to retrace her steps, find the car
she must have been hurled from. He follows her in the truck for fifty
yards, then jerks on the brake, leaves the motor running for the light,

throws open the door, and takes off after her. The dog is looking, though, for one specific person, one familiar scent from all the smells assaulting her, knows whoever is running behind does not belong to her. They cross the bridge over the Santa Cruz, the dry river whose ghost returns in the form of a trickle of treated sewage every night. Sam stops in the middle of the bridge, his breath burning his lungs, and leans over the railing. He waits for his breathing to slow, then lifts his head again and turns. He's crazy to be running, and he knows it. The dog has stopped twenty yards ahead, watching him. In the distance, the headlights of the truck shine, steady as the eyes of an animal, unblinking. And then the dog turns away and trots off beyond the range of light.

❖ He makes his way back to the truck and climbs in. He drives slowly and in another mile the lights of Abner's Bar draw him like a signal into the bay of the parking lot. The truck lurches over the dry potholes and comes to a stop.

The bartender knows without asking what he wants, which is good, because he can't remember what he used to drink. He shoves the Mexican bottle across the bar—Simpatico, beer as dark as the glass it comes in.

A Yaqui woman sits on a stool near the wall at the end of the bar, her broad, dark face turned down, gazing into the grain of the wood before her as if trying to locate something she dropped into a shallow pool of water. Sam recognizes her—Rosa Molina, the memory of her name somehow intact—the wrangler from Rattlesnake Ranch, his competition in the old days. He's seen her more than once on the trails, leading a string of tourists, pulling them like a child's toy behind her as she stared straight ahead, felt hat pulled low over her eyes.

Over her head in the corner a bug light sizzles blue as wings brush the electric coils. Blue lightning. The more he drinks, the more the lightning seems to come from her, a power she can't contain within the bounds of her body. Sam stares at her, transfixed. He lifts his fourth bottle in salutation. "*Encantado,*" he says. The word surfaces

in his mind, fluid, accurate, a gift from another language taken back
by his own tongue.

❖ Hannah opens her eyes. Coyotes call and their hysterical, almost
human cries echo in the box canyon behind the house. She gets up
from the bed, steps onto the cool terra-cotta floor. Her once-brown
hair looks completely gray in the mirror, but her body, she notes, is
still slender and smooth as if forty-five years have no more than
glanced at her. She's surprised at the smoothness, half expects the
accumulation of tension to show itself as indelible ridges on her skin.

She showers and dresses, walks out into the eighty-degree night
air. Hannah climbs the corral fence and sits there, keeping an eye out
for the headlights of the truck. She looks out over the desert again.
It is a place full of spiny things that thrive on harsh conditions, things
that don't want to be touched.

She waits there long enough for the saguaro's shadow to length-
en in the moonlight, the shadows of its needles sharpening too. Sam
is not coming home any time soon. The phone in the barn is mute,
the night filled with radio music from Nogales, Spanish songs. For
the first time since that long vigil the night of his fall it occurs to her
that Sam may have exceeded some limit within himself that won't
let him come home. She knows where he is—less than three miles
away as the crow flies.

She could sit here all night weighing it out, containing herself,
waiting yet another time for him to come back in all senses. But
Hannah feels a force building within herself like dam-trapped water
finally greater than the brace of earth that has held it back for so
long.

She saddles the mare, glad she has to ride, that it will take nearly
an hour rather than the minutes it would take to drive. Her time
together with Sam is a measuring tape stretched taut and straight
between them—anything could break it.

The traffic on the road is frequent these days, so she takes
the longer way through the arroyos. Hannah forces her hands to

hold the reins lightly and lets the horse walk, to take its own sweet time.

❖ A need comes slowly to Sam's mind. He wants to dance with Rosa Molina. He has seen her people dance—always the men—at Easter. All night they dance beneath a *ramada,* the women cross-legged on the floor as the deer dancer moves, wary as the deer he signifies, wearing a rack of antlers twined with flowers.

Rosa looks at him, at the meaning in his extended hand, shrugs at the inevitability of it and rises from her stool to join him. It's a slow dance and she's no good at following him. They are nearly the same age though their paths would not have crossed as children—she most likely from the reservation at Old Pascua, he always with the width and breadth of his own land around him.

Her skin is warm, her hair fragrant with dust, creosote, recent rain. The top of her dark head comes only to his chest. Her hands are toughened by the constant friction of bridle leather. The nearness of her, the familiar smells on a stranger make him unspeakably sad. They move in place, mostly, not exactly dancing so much as leaning against each other. A stream of quarters keeps them going and when the music finally plays itself out it takes the equivalent of half a song before they stop moving.

Hannah finds them like that. She stands in the doorway, unsure of the meaning of the picture before her, if it has anything to do with her at all. She stays there, as if standing on an X taped to the floor.

It's a long minute before he sees her. Hannah counts four deaths, four flashes of lightning on the bug lamp before he connects his sight to her line of vision. Rosa pulls away and makes her way back to the bar, her back straight, her hands gloved in the back pockets of her jeans as if guiding herself forward from behind. She finishes her beer standing, but drinks it slowly, with great deliberateness, sets the bottle down and leaves.

Sam shrugs and looks away but stays where he is. Hannah moves toward him, her boot heels making a hard sound on the floor.

"Come home, Sam," she says. It is not a command or a punishment, nor is it a plea. He shakes his head no.

"What do you want then?"

He turns and walks back to the bar, moves his beer from the small white cocktail napkin branded with a damp ring from the sweating bottle. He takes a ballpoint pen from his shirt pocket, clicks it several times before it works. He writes on the back side of the napkin. She watches him in amazement. It had never occurred to her that he could speak by writing. Why didn't he do this before?

She glances at him quickly before she reads what he's written. She can read nothing in his face so she looks down again. The blue ink blurs into the cottony paper, but the words are still legible.

"Why are you here? I thought you didn't know me anymore."

She turns the napkin over, picks up the pen from the bar, and writes inside the damp circle.

"You're not that easy to forget—just like that."

She shoves the napkin toward him and he writes back.

"I've forgotten a lot of things. Just like that. Maybe you should too."

He stabs the final period hard into the napkin and it tears a hole through to the other side.

She wants him to fight instead of letting everything slip away but there's not enough space left on the napkin to get it all across. "You didn't forget how to dance, or how to write," she scribbles. It's neutral written down, without inflection. If she said it out loud it would be an accusation.

The napkin is running out of room, crowded with their conversation. Hannah wants to keep it going—all of a sudden there seems to be a lot to say.

"Like riding a bicycle," he writes. Then he grins. He's finally gotten in the last word.

"Dance with me then," she says out loud with an unmistakable "Prove it" tone in her voice. She lifts herself from the bar stool, mimes the stick figure that she had scratched on the rock that morning, and in this dark bar it seems not a gesture of surrender but of a woman holding out her hands.

But he's not taking her up on it, at least not yet. He wants time to flex the fingers of this slight upper hand. He motions for the bartender, points at his beer, then holds up two fingers. The bartender nods and places two bottles on the bar with a glass for Hannah. She leaves it untouched and moves to the dance floor, begins to dance alone.

Sam shades his eyes and watches her. There is no light to speak of, just the red glow of a Cerveza sign in the window by the door. No sun, just the glare of old desire.

Sam rises from the bar stool and walks stiffly onto the dance floor and stops in front of her, legs braced as against a sudden wind. He tightens his body, holds his arms in a rigid L shape around her, his mind a sudden blank with the effort of grace. Still, he feels a wave of yearning, though it's no longer exactly clear to him what that is anymore or if Hannah's its source.

Hannah remembers the feel of his flannel shirt, the small, re-assuring pressure of the pearl button that day in the green field in the Chiricahuas. Slowly, she brings her face to rest it there again. Her touch makes him flinch and she pictures the mare's shoulder rippling to rid herself of flies. Hannah pulls back and looks up.

He takes his hands back, shoves them both in his pockets, rocks back on his boot heels.

"Now what?" she says.

He doesn't answer. He cocks his head toward the door. "Let's go," the gesture says, in any language.

❖ The mare stands as still as a statue. Sam laces his fingers into a stirrup and Hannah steps lightly into his hands. She climbs on.

He takes hold of the reins and for a minute they both hold on to the line, neither willing to let go first. She relaxes her hands slightly and he feels the slack. He takes it up and gently pulls the reins over the mare's head. The hinges on the bit move, squeaking as they slowly turn.

The moon is high, seven-eighths full, and flawed. The desert seems more full of shadows than it ever does in daylight. They pass the sign at the edge of the road: Ranchettes—from $59,500. They walk past the bulldozers and graders, past the piles of rebar and conduit, and find their way down the slope to the wash—a groove that remains unchanged despite the stripping of the land around it. Water will flow there once or twice a year during the most spectacular storms.

Neither of them notices, but a dog trails them at a distance that will satisfy both its caution and curiosity.

From where she sits she can see the straightness in the back of the man before her, how his shoulder blades curve beneath his shirt. He walks ahead, holding on to her and the horse through the lines. He senses, as if he can see them, Hannah's hands, free, resting easy on her thighs, the rolling stride of the horse gently rocking her.

❖ *The Ways We Hear about It*

In the summer of '63 we moved to Donner Lake, California, when my father, tired of being a widower for five years, found himself a new wife. I was just thirteen, my sister Jude nearly ten. We were a family with more to get used to about each other than we ever dreamed, and we had a standard joke that we'd better learn to get along or we'd end up like the Donner party for which the lake was named—a band of settlers trapped in snow who ended up devouring each other.

And we did learn to get along, but we were set in our ways, too. Grieving had made us stoic and solitary and we didn't let anyone into our lives easily. My father's new wife, Linda, must have felt she was set down in the midst of a strange, silent brood. She'd come from California, firstborn in a raucous, close-knit family of ten in which you had to shout to be heard at the supper table, where you grappled for the very covers on the bed.

I tried to imagine her, curled up with several of her sisters, listening to her father sing them to sleep. Our family slept at such distances from each other I couldn't even hear Jude's nightmare shouts or my father's snoring through the walls. At first I thought Linda could save us, that her California exclamations would crowd out our New England dirge, but we were a force to be reckoned with, and slowly, as in the great empty calm after a solar system explodes, we inched toward new orbits at a safer distance from the sun.

Years later, my sister and I both married men that believed we could be more vulnerable if we only tried harder, and they quickly came up against the solid buttress of all our silent defenses, shields as thick as earthen walls that kept us at a constant, tolerable temperature. Words might have gotten through, but none of us knew what to say. Jude got stoned; I got sullen. We kept out of each other's hair. We didn't tell my father and Linda that our marriages were in trouble; if they noticed anything at all, they kept what they considered a respectful distance, believing that if we needed help we would simply say so, though we had no precedent or practice, no earthly idea how to begin.

❖ Christmas, 1988. Jude and I return to Donner Lake in separate cars, on separate days. Actually, she misses Christmas eve altogether, calls in the afternoon to say she'll see us tomorrow. No "sorry," no "because," just "tomorrow."

When she arrives, she makes her entrance high on high heels and cocaine. My father and Linda think she is just happy, just a little wound up. We are surprised that she has arrived at all. Last year her place at the table stayed set for two days until Linda finally folded up the place mat and put it away without comment.

So here she is, skinny and wired and flushed with sudden goodwill and apprehension. She is strung between several poles, taut as an E string on a new guitar.

She kicks off her shoes first thing. Darts between us, bestowing hugs so light we can scarcely feel her arms around us. Turns her cheek to our kisses.

"The snow is so great!" she says, waving her arms at the picture window where the pines and camellias droop, and I understand why she likes it, the white veil that falls equally over everything. It's a fresh start, no tracks or smudges, and she'll be gone before it melts. Already I can see her tire tracks tomorrow morning curving away from the house, cutting two dark furrows in the perfect snow.

"Well," she says, rubbing her hands, shedding her coat like a skin. "I could use a hot toddy." She turns to me. "How about you, Ceese?" She always shortens my name. Everyone else calls me Cecelia. She rolls her eyes. "Oh, right, you don't drink. I forgot."

She didn't forget. She just needs to draw the line straight off, a liquid boundary between us.

"How was the drive?" my father asks. It's always his opening line, as if we have to pay homage to the trajectory to the house before we can comprehend we're all in the same room again.

"Made it in two and a half hours," Jude says.

"Lord, Lord, Lord," he says, shaking his head in wonderment at this daughter of his, trying to understand the speed of her life. "It takes me at least four to get to you."

"The beemer likes to gallop," she says, lifting her glass to it. Her BMW sits poised in the driveway, unbelievably red in the stark white world, so hot still from sustained high gear that I imagine I hear snowflakes sizzling on its gleaming hood.

Linda picks up Jude's high heels, places them side by side by the front door. They stand absurdly at attention and look as if they might walk away any minute of their own inclination. She turns back to Jude.

"How's Stephen?" she asks her. "We're so sorry he couldn't come this year."

"He's fine, just fine," she says, taking a long pull on her hot buttered rum. "He's at his folks'—you know, the Super Glue family."

I know that she and Stephen have recently separated though my parents do not. Rites of passage in our family are never communicated directly but deduced from significant details that pile up eventually into facts when they are too numerous to ignore any longer.

"How's that job?" my father asks her. This is always his second question and will soon lead to many other work-related questions that hang off the original subject like a complex diagrammed sentence. Work is what he really wants to talk about, not Stephen.

"For God's sake, Dad," I say. "Let her sit down for two minutes before you start Twenty Questions."

He leans forward in his chair, agitated by my interruption, and swings his long legs off the hassock.

"I'm just asking her about her work, Cecelia. The fact that you're no longer gainfully employed doesn't mean other people aren't." He leans back in his chair, having put me in my proper place. I might have known he'd be annoyed at me for quitting my job at the newspaper to be a freelance photographer, but this is the first I hear about it.

Jude sighs, "The job's OK. Just got a raise, and they're sending me to England in March for a month to work with the project manager there."

My father has never worked for a corporation in his life, being stubbornly self-employed, and I had hoped he'd be secretly proud of me. But the fact that Jude works for Kodak never ceases to impress him. Her entry into that world is tantamount in his mind to infiltrating the KGB and returning with exotic and indisputable secrets.

Linda disappears into the kitchen through one swinging door and reappears out the other carrying a stack of coasters.

"I got these at the church bazaar—the old lady down the street made them. Aren't they just the limit?"

She holds one out to Jude like an offering. It's her way of intervening, of keeping my father from taking over the conversation. The coasters have purple daisies with yellow faces painted on them. The faces are intended, I'm sure, to be smiling, but the eyes are drawn so wide they simply look stunned.

"Amazing," Jude says, and giggles. "Don't start hanging out with church ladies too much, Linda, or you'll wind up on a committee—after that, it's all downhill."

We all laugh. It's a nice moment. The turkey is roasting, the oven timer ticking in an unhurried way, the snow is falling lightly, benevolently; strains of "Good King Wenceslas" leak out of my father's portable radio. My sister's stockinged feet are curled beneath her and there's a run sliding slowly down her calf. Linda hums along with the radio, slightly off-key. I take a mental picture of it—a picture I will wonder about when I come across it years later, a moment so brief and perfect we would hardly remember we were there, nearly happy, all our losses gone to ground.

But an enlargement would reveal this: the set of my sister's mouth as if she couldn't, without considerable effort, think of what to say next. And myself? I'm the one with arms folded a little too tightly across the chest as if to protect myself from a sudden blow. My father is looking, not at any of us, but at his watch, preparing to turn up the news on the radio which will obliterate our conversation with headlines and the crackle of foreign correspondence. Linda is looking at my father with a tolerance and tenderness for his habits, though Jude and I can both vividly recall their heated arguments after they first got married and the way Linda would slam the front door behind her, get in the Buick Roadmaster and drive too fast around the neighborhood until she either ran out of gas or her frustration at his implacable will simmered down enough to come home.

Just behind us are the framed snapshots of our marriages—Jude's and mine—already or soon to be past tense. Our bridal smiles are so hopefully naive in the belief that we could start over, that the word "everlasting" might yet apply to us. And our husbands: boys in suits and new mustaches, not dreaming yet how miserable they were capable of making us or we them, or how we would all hang on past the long string of bitter ends until the chasm got so wide we couldn't stretch ourselves across it anymore.

❖ My father turns up the news, and, as usual, he hasn't got it tuned in quite right. All the S's hiss and Jude slides down deeper into her wingbacked chair, covering her ears. Linda shouts from the kitchen, but it's just wordless sound that can't compete against the cease-fire in Jerusalem or the derailment in Birmingham. So she stands in the doorway, broadcasting directly to Jude.

"Why don't you freshen up before dinner—we're almost ready."

"I'm beyond freshening," Jude mutters.

My father snaps the radio off. Jude sighs—a deep, drawn-out exhalation. She stands up but she's coming apart, her thin composure like a hem unraveling faster than she can stitch it up. She takes her purse into the bathroom. When I walk by the closed door I can hear the sound of a razor blade ticking on her compact mirror. Anything I might say to try to bring her back will only be unintelligible sound, muffled by the door.

❖ When our mother died, no one spoke of it. Neighbors brought casseroles for days, as if sorrow made us hungry and we had forgotten how to feed ourselves. My father decided that at eight I was too young to go to the funeral, too young to stand by the headstone and read all the letters of her name. He also decided that four was too young for Jude to even be told about it, and swore me to silence. A year later, I heard her crying in her room, which was next to mine, and I knew what she was crying about. I got down on the floor by the heating vent and stroked it like a harp with my fingernail—once for hello—to get her attention. It was the secret signal we used at night, when we wanted to whisper through the vents, exchange secrets like spies. She stopped crying when she heard my signal, then got down on the floor to listen. "What's the matter, Jude?" I asked.

She answered between choking sobs, "Carol and Frankie were shouting 'Nah nah, your mother's dead' and I yelled back at them 'She is NOT!' because she isn't, is she, Ceese?"

I played the thick strings of the gray metal harp again, and it zinged and echoed all the way down the silver ducts to the dark furnace in the basement and back again.

"She really is," I whispered, because we tried to tell the truth here, and it seemed to quiet her. From the other side of the wall she answered, strumming, her small fingers making the softest music. Two long and one short: good-bye.

❖ The electric carving knife zizzes through the steaming breast of turkey, and thin slices fold over and fall to the platter like thick white petals from a heavy flower.

"That's a terrible sound," Jude says to my father. "Hurry up, will you?"

He holds the knife above the turkey and it quivers and buzzes like an overturned beetle.

"It takes the time it takes, and in my decrepit state this could take a while. Just relax, young lady."

Relax! I laugh out loud and Jude shoots me a "just you shut up" look.

I unfold my napkin with a sigh. It's going to be an ordeal of a holiday, and I can feel Jude's frenetic energy, her barely contained edginess building, as if we shared a main artery like Siamese twins and could anticipate each other's flinches, twinges, and yawns. But that is only half true. She has more or less successfully anesthetized herself, screened out my pulse, which must sound to her like it does nothing but compete against her own. In my house, I could retreat to the darkroom, seal myself off and concentrate on something I had a modicum of control over: time and light and the subtle variations of each. But here, I'm unprotected against each surge in her fast-fluxing mood, and, like too much light on high-speed film, everything I see is overexposed.

She eats tiny nibbles, stirs her food around on her plate, creates a vortex pattern with her mashed potatoes and gravy.

Linda heaps more cranberry sauce on my father's plate though he didn't ask for it, then heaps some more on her own. The red juice leaks into the gravy. "You're still too skinny, Jude. Are you on a diet or what?"

"No, I'm not on a diet," Jude says, which doesn't really explain anything.

Linda moves right along, not skipping a beat. "How about going to the midnight service?" She looks expectant and excited, as if she's offered up a completely original idea, but she says it every year and every year my father thinks of a reason why we shouldn't go.

This year, he says, "It's too cold. Too cold and too far."

"Ed, you're turning into an old coot, you know it?"

"Who are you calling an old coot?"

"Old fart, not coot. Sorry."

Oh God, here it comes. But she grins at him, and, amazingly, he grins back. Jude steals a glance at me and raises her eyebrows as if to say, "Do you know these two people?" We'd heard so many hurled insults and prolonged nagging between them, plenty of two-fisted fighting. But when had they learned there was humor just on the other side, that, without capitulation, one of them could turn it half a degree toward the absurd and actually laugh about it? Is this what happens when you get old? Suddenly, I wish that Jude and I were decades older, all our edges worn smooth.

It's dark when we finish eating and our reflection deepens in the picture window—a medieval scene: candles and picked carcasses, all of us pushed back from the table in heavy, carved chairs. Linda's face, closest to the candles, is the only one of us in color. Those of us related by blood are half in shadow, blurred together in a common dusk, our features oddly congruent and overlapping like an accidental double exposure that looks as if the photographer planned it that way all along.

❖ Linda creates a whirlwind of table clearing and takes her last but hardly hidden helpings from serving spoons when she scrapes the leftovers into Tupperware containers. It's her favorite way to eat, and I've always appreciated the obvious pleasure she takes in it. I can almost imagine her as a little girl in the midst of her huge family, savoring the dinner longest because she licked the spoons.

Jude nearly jumps out of her skin when Linda flips the garbage disposal switch. Her hands grip the sink and she closes her eyes.

"I'll finish up here," Linda says. "You girls go for a walk, why don't you. The moon's up—it'll be lovely."

I look at Jude and she shrugs. "Yeah, OK. Thanks, Linda."

We rummage in the hall closet for the old winter coats we still keep here. We bundle up, and, mitten-bound, scarf-wrapped, Vibram-soled, we clump outside like astronauts weighted against zero gravity.

We walk in silence for half a block, but my head is racing, trying to think of something to say. The snow is blue streaked with navy shadows of trees. The moon is a lens of ice in the black, wind-cleared sky.

"Jude, remember how we used to make a sled track in the backyard—I'd turn the sled over, pile some logs inside the runners. You'd sit on top and I'd haul it all down the hill."

I pictured myself from her perspective on the sled—a shape bent forward, straining like a horse in the harness.

Her voice seems to come from a great distance. "I remember. We had a Flexible Flyer. My boots were always coming unsnapped. The snot froze on my face. You always had Kleenex."

Snow squinches beneath our boots. The living rooms along our street flicker with television and Christmas lights, some erratic and patternless, some a measured blink. Only one house still has a black and white set—blue light dances on the white walls of the room, and as we pass someone draws the curtains as if they felt us looking into their lives.

We come to the cul-de-sac at the end of the street and stop.

"What do you make of Dad and Linda these days—they seem to get a kick out of each other," Jude says. She spreads her arms and scuffs her feet along, making a snaky, continuous track with all her footprints running together, drawing a lopsided circle around us.

"Dad's either getting more relaxed or getting more scared," I say.

"Scared of what?"

"Didn't Linda tell you?"

She turns toward me. Our hoods are like blinders, forcing us to face each other directly in order to see.

"Tell me what?"

"He's having prostate surgery after the holidays."

"Goddammit—no one tells me anything. How'd you find out? No, don't tell me, you probably saw it on Linda's calendar and had to ask her yourself. Jesus!"

She slaps her mittened hands against her sides with a muffled whack.

"No, she didn't tell me. I just happened to call the day he saw the doctor and it came out as an 'Oh, by the way' statement, along with the weather and plans for remodeling the bathroom."

"You mean we all just sat there at dinner tonight and no one said a word about it!"

"Since when do they talk about their problems with us? Why do you expect things to be different? Anyway, I called his doctor. He said it's very common with men Dad's age. I really think it'll be OK."

I scoop up a handful of snow, think about eating some, think better of it. I pack it into a lopsided ball and throw it at a stop sign.

"For that matter, Jude, we don't talk with them either."

"That's because there's nothing to tell." Jude scoops up her own wad of snow and throws it at the sign. The snowball hits the *S* and sticks there, obscuring the top of its curve so it looks like an upside-down question mark from another language.

"Not worth saying out loud," she continues. "Boring," she concludes, and throws another snowball, missing the sign.

"Look—I know something's happened between you and Stephen."

"Then you read it in the *Chronicle*—you didn't hear it from me. Or did he tell you?"

She doesn't know what to do with her hands. She's coming down. She can't stand still. "Look—when you went through your divorce that's all I heard about for weeks. I'm not going to bore you with mine."

It hurts, though I shouldn't be as surprised as I am—I always thought we were closer then—she took me to see *Tristan and Isolde* on my birthday that year and we both sat there and cried.

"You seemed sympathetic at the time."

"Sympathy isn't enough for you, Ceese—you want *empathy*—hand-holding, tearful embraces, reunion. I haven't got any left—used it all up." Her arms flail against the air for punctuation, then fall to her sides again. But she's not finished, not yet.

"Listen, Ceese, I would never let myself get as completely out of control as you did—you just fell apart."

I'm so taken aback I just say the first thing that comes into my head. "I suppose you're holding your life up as an example of being in control! Hey, if I could snort a hundred bucks up my nose and forget myself for half an hour I would have done it by now, be doing it all day long just like you. I'd be delighted! I'd be getting off cheap! But it doesn't do it for me, Jude, it just makes everything worse. I wish I could just stop thinking once in a while, but I can't."

"Then I feel sorry for you." She turns and starts to walk back toward the house.

I lunge after her, grab her by the shoulder, but before I can say anything she takes a swing at me and then all four feet go out from under us and we're rolling like a single, frenzied animal in the snow.

"Don't you talk to me like that—you take that back right now!" I yell.

"What are you, five years old?" She pounds on my shoulder with her fist.

And I want to be five, or less than five if I can get away with it, want to be wild with pure, unadulterated rage, to kick and scream and spit, tell her she hurts, tell her to just stop it, tell her to stop disapproving of everything I do.

But I'm not five. I'm damn near forty and my own anger scares me at least as much as hers.

"I want the kind of sister I can talk to!" I shout. She jerks her body away from me, kicking. I roll her on her stomach, pin her down with my leg, push her face deep into the snow. She goes limp for a minute, then surges up, twists herself around, grabs an end of my knotted muffler and yanks it until I can hardly breathe. She leans close. Her breath comes at me, a heated cloud, warm on my face.

"OK—are you listening? Know that weekend you went to Mendocino when you and Tim first split up? He wanted to spend the night with me." She lets go of me, believing she has finally pronounced the last word.

"Tell me something I don't already know." My voice is low, but clearly audible. All I can feel is the snow melting into my knees. "You're too late, Jude. His best friend let it slip a year ago. On the telephone, Jude!"

She sits back on her heels, staring, but I can't see her face. "So why didn't you say something to me?" she asks.

"Why didn't *you*? I shouldn't have to say anything. I was afraid that if I did, I'd lose you too."

I stand up. My knees shake with cold. Haven't I been waiting for this, haven't I longed to hear myself say this out loud, for her to say something back? What I really want is the safety of the heating vent, a screen through which we can whisper and be forgiven for what we have to say.

At the end of the block, along the main road, yellow lights skitter across the snow, and for one ridiculous moment I'm sure it's the sheriff, that the neighbors heard us shouting and called the cops. Then we hear the roar of the plow, scraping all the way down to the asphalt, and it leaves a dark strip flanked by a wake of churned-up snow. We watch it pass the stop sign at the bottom of the hill and stay still until it's out of sight. Neither of us knows what comes next. I sit down again, several feet away from her.

The wind fills the trees, threads itself through the weft of pine needles. I hear the sound of a car behind us and I know without looking, by the chugging idle and the thunk of chains on the wheel rims, that it's my father's ancient Fairlane station wagon. Jude and I sit, blinded in the high beam's glare. He comes alongside of us. The power window lowers with a muffled shriek.

"You girls all right? What in hell are you doing sitting in the middle of the road?"

"Just sitting, Dad. It's OK. Really. It's OK," Jude says and her voice sounds strangely calm.

"Well then," he says through the window. A long pause. The car nearly stalls, he revs hard. "If I thought I could get up again I might get down there in the road with you. Your mother would, that much I know. She loved the snow."

He hasn't talked about her in years and all of a sudden it seems she's right here, among us.

"You want a ride?" We shake our heads. "Just don't catch cold," he says. The window rises. The car shifts into drive with a resounding clunk and he slowly makes a wide swerve around us until he turns completely around in the cul-de-sac. We turn and watch his taillights until they disappear altogether.

Jude pushes back her hood and puts her head down on her knees. She wraps her arms around her legs, rocks slowly back and forth.

I push my own hood back to feel the sting of cold air on my scalp. I crawl over to her, then stop. I sit down, press my back to hers and we face in opposite directions. We bang our heads together by accident when she straightens up. "Ow!" and "Sorry," she says.

"It's all right," I say. We lean lightly against each other. When I turn my head a little bit, I think I can feel her hair against my cheek, though it could just as easily be my own. In the distance, I can see the outline of the Sierra, the break of Donner Pass where those settlers never dreamed the taste of communion would haunt them all their lives. And then I see, as if from a height, the tire tracks my father left, their lopsided circumference, a lasso flung so loose and wide we hardly heard it singing through the air until it was all around us.

❖ Recovery

I make my way down from Dolores Street, down the hill that is too steep for a sidewalk. I descend the long flight of stairs like a child, watching my feet find each step. I'm almost in front of my apartment building before I notice that the entryway is blocked by a wall of packing boxes. Someone is moving in, or out. The door is propped open and a tide of paper—flyers, newspapers, wrappers—has drifted into the dim foyer. A woman's head appears above the cardboard barrier, then disappears like a bird in a carnival shooting gallery. The head appears again, then turns. She smiles at me.

"I'm moving into number five." She steps out from behind the boxes and I feel relieved to see the rest of her.

"I'm in number six, right across the hall. I'm Georgia Brecker." I extend my hand.

"Anna Lanier," she says.

We are the same height and coloring and are both wearing identical skirts made of a Southwestern print; from a distance we could easily be mistaken for each other.

"We could post a schedule in the hall for wearing these skirts," I say, hoping she has a sense of humor.

The laughter between us seems an easy thing to come by but there is something unsettling about the resemblance. I think about the way a kitten hisses the first time it sees itself in a mirror. I think about those double takes I've done more than once, not immediately recognizing my own reflection as it turned to face me from a store window and hurried on. At those moments I'm always left with the notion that I've just seen myself for the first time the way other people do, that I've caught a fleeting glimpse of a woman stripped of her usual assurances, vulnerable and strangely out of context in the glare of broad daylight.

In the days that follow, I see her lighted window across the airshaft, a window that has been dark for weeks and now is almost naked in its brightness. Through it, I can see the walls of her kitchen, the pictures that appear one at a time, the jars of spice above the stove, the wok on top of the refrigerator, until one day when I look out of my window into hers to see what else has materialized in the room, my view is blocked by a lace curtain she's put there sometime during the night.

I feel shut out. I've been imagining how the kitchen doors, which face each other across the back stairwell, could be open in the mornings, how we might walk back and forth in our robes and slippers, a mug of coffee in hand. We'd be familiar with each other's rooms, and have long conversations about German poetry, the unarticulated emotions of men, the Manhattanization of San Francisco. But I wait until I get a specific invitation. I don't want to scare her away, to seem like someone who will take up too much room in the life she has been living alone.

Two weeks pass before Anna knocks on my door. "I've just made a pot of coffee—want to join me?"

"I'd love to. I'll be over in a minute."

"I'll leave the door open, just come in when you're ready."

She's in the kitchen when I walk into her apartment. I quickly scan the bookshelf in the hallway. It's like reading the backs of my own books: Rilke, Hass, Gallagher. And on the wall, the same O'Keeffe print: the pale gray shell rising above a hot, scarlet desert.

Two years earlier I had lived in that same apartment before the quieter one across the hall became available. I was going through a divorce at the time and I remembered lying awake so many nights listening to cars grinding up the Twenty-fifth Street hill. I was sleepless with grief and invaded by the noise of a world I had become separate from. And now another woman has arrived alone from what I imagine to be some recent loss. I study the room which looks so much like mine and feel again that sense of flight, that landing on the top floor of an old apartment building rooted with redwood timbers, a building like a tree that sways and shakes from the wind off the bay, literally creaking in earthquakes. No matter what we put here—furniture, flowers, handwoven rugs—there is still a persistent echo that lives in the walls.

"Cream or sugar or both?"

"Black," I answer. As I walk out of the living room a cassette tape on her stereo shelf catches my eye, "Meditation before Surgery," and as I move toward the brightness of the kitchen I look carefully at her, as if some part of her might have been cut away already. Through her kitchen window I see my own—curtainless, exposed, the type on the O'Keeffe print clearly readable from where I stand.

I'm trying to think of something to say. I point to the drawers beneath the counter. "I used to keep my underwear and socks in there because I couldn't afford a dresser when I first came."

"You mean you lived *here?*"

"I moved because the street noise really got to me after a while."

She nods. A picture above her sink pulls my attention and I lean closer for a better look. It is a yellow field of wheat divided by a crossroads as straight as a part in a head of thick, blond hair. Looming in the distance at the edge of the field a summer storm—and a sky so bruised with clouds it looks as if it will pour any minute, flood the crossroads and flatten the stalks of wheat below.

She stands next to me, and as we look at the storm in silence it seems to push the light out of the room, as if its dark weather can't be contained for very long within the small wooden frame.

"My life's been like that lately—like that picture," she says. "Things looming in the background, coming closer."

We make our way to the couch. I want to ask her what she means, but let her take her time.

"I had breast cancer five years ago and had a mastectomy." I try not to look at her chest as she speaks. "Six months ago it came back, after four years of remission. I had to have a hysterectomy."

"Are you all right now?" The question sounds as ridiculous as the unintended rhyme in her operations.

"In theory. As long as I take my little white pills, but it seems such a tiny army to overcome the Vandals and the Huns."

I look at her long, lean body, at the graceful way she sits, her legs tucked perfectly beneath her, and it's hard to imagine that inside she is so constantly under siege.

I tell her about my divorce, the long process of becoming a separate person again, but the pain which had been so acute seems suddenly dissipated in this room by the large words of surgical procedures that hang in the air above us. We finish the coffee slowly, we say we will get together again soon.

❖ We don't see a lot of each other. There isn't much time because Anna has every spare minute of her life scheduled, from reviewing new theater productions, to fund-raising for repertory companies, to teaching children improvisational dance. I slide new poems I've written under her door and occasionally we have coffee in the morning, sometimes at her place, sometimes at mine. There are times when I notice that she looks tired, pale. I wonder if she ever wakes at night, afraid. I wonder if she would ever call me if she was afraid, ask me to come over and just sit with her for a while until the light comes through the windows and city noises fill the streets below.

I think about my mother, who was Anna's age when she died of cancer. How, forbidden by hospital rules to visit her because I was only eight, I waited up every night for my father to come back from seeing her. I would run down the stairs and I would ask the same question: "How is she?" I always got the same vague answer. "Better," my father would say in a tired voice, not looking at me as he turned to go downstairs where he slept in a small room on a rollaway bed. The big room they had shared together was too large, too expansive for what was becoming the narrowing down of his life. We were a family that was shrinking and not getting any closer, getting used to living with less, while abundance drifted slowly outside our field of vision.

❖ Anna calls on a Sunday morning. "There's no fog for a change— let's go to the beach."

We drive out Lucas Valley Road to Point Reyes. The long grass on the rounded hills that has been bleached blond all summer has grown out at the roots and returned to its natural color. We stop at a bakery in Inverness and buy two cappuccinos in paper cups and a pile of pastries which the baker puts in a big pink box and ties with string. We drive to Kehoe Beach through the dairies and herds of black and white cows grazing on the steep cliffs above the shoreline. There are no trees except for the occasional cypress, its leaves and branches blown permanently backward at an unnatural angle by the constant wind. We walk down the cow path to the beach through fields of purple and pale yellow lupine, taking turns carrying the pink box.

The beach is nearly deserted and we find a sheltered place in the dunes. The foam has subsided in the cappuccinos, melted down into the rich espresso. It is still hot and bitter-strong and warms us as we sit in the cool sand. The steady wind pulls our hair back from our foreheads. We devour the pastries one by one.

"I've been thinking of moving out here this summer," I tell her. She looks up at me, startled. "I'd really like to get out of the city.

What I spend in parking tickets alone would finance a cottage in Inverness."

"Oh *no,*" she says and I'm surprised at the distress in her voice. "I've gotten used to the idea of you being right across the hall. It makes me feel safer somehow."

I know she doesn't mean safe from burglars. Maybe she does sleep badly, waking at three or four in the morning when it is both too early and too late to get up. Maybe she listens to her body at these times, to her pulse and her own music, vital and particular. Maybe she listens for sounds of discord, signals from the cells that are either rallying in her defense or betraying her. Maybe she thinks of me, knowing I'm sound asleep across the hall, a mere twenty feet away, and that if she wants to, she can simply knock on my door and wake me.

Seagulls swirl above us on a column of air. I don't talk any more about moving. We both sit facing out to sea. The wind roars in our ears.

❖ "I met a man," she tells me one morning on the back stairway.

"Is he still in there?" I ask, looking over her shoulder through the open door into her apartment.

"God, no. I just met him a few days ago. His name's Miguel—from Nicaragua, but he lives here now and works at the public radio station. I met him at a fund-raiser and at first I thought 'Not my type.' I mean, he's kind of short and round, you know? But I keep thinking of him."

"Well, I'm sure he hasn't forgotten you either."

She grins. We hug each other—two women standing on the back stairs surrounded by mops and brooms and an abandoned aquarium.

Her light is on late that night. In the morning, she comes over and says before she's even come all the way through the door, "I'm scared."

She collapses on the sofa. "What'll he think the first time we make love and I have to undress and he finds out I have only one breast?

What if he can't bear to look at me? What if my cancer scares him away?"

She says 'my cancer' as if it truly belongs to her—some orphan child that has moved in on her and refuses to let go, a child that clings to her with a hunger, needy and fierce. I don't know Miguel, but somehow I feel that coming from a country mutilated by war he won't bat an eye at any scar on her body. I tell her so and for the first time since we met, she cries. I pull a wadded tissue from my bathrobe pocket and hand it to her. I wish I had a picture of us: Anna in her purple bathrobe, me in blue, sunlight falling through the bay windows onto our uncombed hair.

❖ Miguel stays with Anna several nights a week and although I see less of her we still manage a few minutes alone in the morning. Sometimes she leaves Miguel singing in the shower while she sits with me on my couch. My two cats rub against our legs and she reads my latest poems.

❖ On a weeknight when Anna is previewing a new play I'm at home, ironing—something I never do. The ironing board belongs to Anna but it lives between the two apartments in the back stairway next to the aquarium. When I finish ironing I can't get the board to collapse again. I fuss with it for several minutes and, completely frustrated, give up. When I see Anna's kitchen light go on I knock on her door.

"Is there some special trick to getting the ironing board down?"

"No. It usually behaves itself."

"Well, it's acting up tonight. Come on, I need your help."

She follows me into my kitchen, walks over and does the customary things one usually does with a functioning ironing board. But this one is stubborn. We turn it upside down and it looks like some absurd, overturned insect with blue legs sticking up in the air. We sit on the floor and tug at the jammed release lever. I get a knife out of the drawer and we poke and pry until the point breaks off. We begin attacking the ironing board with an arsenal of scissors, screwdrivers, and spatulas, whatever we can grab out of the drawer, but a systematic, mechanical approach goes right out the window and soon we are banging out a wild rhythm on its metal frame.

"Maybe if we got a whip," I suggest hopefully.

My cats, thoroughly alarmed at all the noise, escape to the relative safety of the bedroom.

"This is a symbol of something," she says.

"Let me guess—it's the Achilles' heel of the entire women's movement."

We lean against each other, shaking with laughter.

"Well, what we need then is a man!" Anna says. "I mean, they're never around when you need them for the truly important things in life."

We roll away from each other until we're both lying on the floor, our laughter completely out of control, unstoppable. And then, laughter subsides as we lie there, staring up at the cracked ceiling into the white heat of a hundred-watt bulb. The refrigerator switches off with a shudder and the silence that follows is sudden and complete.

She feels along the floor until she finds my hand and holds it as if we're in the dark.

"It came back," she says, almost in a whisper.

"What did?" I ask, still looking up at the ceiling.

"The Vandals and the Huns. The clouds at the back of the picture. They're camping out in my lungs."

We lie in the bare, bright light with the scissors, the screwdriver, the spatula, and the spoons strewn around us. I squeeze her hand tightly as if I can send something down the veins, some message that might matter, some energy that could shift the weight of an unmovable stone. We hold on. After a while, the cats come in, trusting the room again, and lie down in the narrow space between us.

❖ Rain Dance at Blue Cloud

The summer I turned thirteen was the same summer my mother, for reasons she couldn't explain in the note she left on the kitchen table, ran away, and my father left me in Custer, South Dakota, with friends while he drove on to California to try to bring her back home. I wanted to go with him, but as it always happened with my parents, their troubles had no particular beginning and no definite end and were shouted out privately in rooms behind closed doors. Now I would simply have to wait for them to work it out together or for my father to come back alone.

My father was taking me to the Blue Cloud Inn, where I was to work for wages and my room and board. My parents had stayed at that inn on their honeymoon fourteen years before. Old friends of the family owned and ran this small resort near the Black Hills where tourists stayed on their way to Montana to see the Little Big Horn. After the drab flatlands of central Michigan, everything in South Dakota seemed named for a color.

"Why is it called the Blue Cloud?" I asked him as we turned in at the painted sign. "Clouds are really white."

He thought a minute. "I guess people think of them as blue."

I wondered about this. It seemed significant that things could be so deliberately confused, that you could see things in a certain way just because you wanted to.

We pulled up in front of a two-story stone lodge with a long front porch lined with green metal lawn chairs. Blue shutters framed the windows and a green lawn fanned out from the house like a skirt, its perimeter lined with the same stones the house was made of.

A woman came to the screen door at the end of the porch. She stood there for a moment before coming out, and through the sun-struck mist of the screen she looked as vague as smoke. She pushed the door with the flat of her hand and it sprang open; she stepped out into the bright sunlight. Her white hair wound around her head and ended in a complicated knot. She wore men's khaki pants, a white shirt with deep pockets over her breasts, salmon-colored flip-flops on her tanned feet. She looked past me to my father, just straightening up from pulling my suitcase out of the back of the station wagon.

"Hugh," she called, and waved. She ran down the steps and clapped my father on the back. He ducked his head in a boyish way that made him look both awkward and pleased. Finally she turned to me and thrust out her hand.

"You must be Rita. I always thought that was such a pretty name."

She gripped my hand, squeezed it hard for a second, then let it go as if it was either too hot or too cold for her liking. I didn't know what to do with it after that. I stuffed it in my pocket so it wouldn't just hang there by my side. Her blue eyes were as bright as glass. A little white shape, like a wisp of fog, flawed her left iris. I felt pinned beneath its scrutiny.

She turned again to my father.

"Hugh—stay for lunch, won't you? You're always in such a god-awful hurry when you pass through here."

For a minute I was afraid he would turn her down and leave me to contend with her disappointment, which might be considerable, but he wiped the sweat off his forehead with the back of his sleeve.

"Sure. Why not?"

He steered me with a hand on my shoulder—a gesture for which I was grateful because I was beginning to feel extra, fading out of view in the straight-down sunlight and heat. We followed her through the screen door into the dark, cool house.

Inside was an enormous kitchen, a black stove with ten or twelve burners and dozens of burnished pots and pans hanging from a rack on the wall. There were three places set at a small round table in an alcove by the bay window—a bright corner in the otherwise gloomy expanse of the room.

She served up sandwiches and pickles, tall glasses of iced tea.

She looked at me when she sat down. "The first guests arrive tomorrow—three couples, one on a honeymoon." She stole a glance at my father, but he didn't see. She bit off a corner of her sandwich, chased it with a big swallow of tea, and continued.

"Rita, we start early at the Blue Cloud. Six o'clock is first call for you. You'll set up the dining room for breakfast. People start drifting in around seven, and the last stragglers come in just before nine. Then there's the clean-up from breakfast, and after that, there's the rooms—just tidying up the ones that are staying on, but a thorough cleaning of the ones that have gone."

I pictured ten enormous beds, all requiring meticulous hospital corners. Hair in bathtub drains not belonging to anyone I knew.

She went on. "Then there's the lunch to get through. After that, the afternoon's yours. Five to eight is dinner, and after that's cleaned up, you're done." She drained her glass of tea and looked right at me. "Think you can handle all that?"

I nodded slowly, uncertain. I must have looked rather solemn because my father laughed—it was good to hear him laugh again, even though it was at my expense—and suddenly I felt overcome with a desperate, unexpressible wish that he would change his mind and take me with him, instead of leaving me behind with a stranger who seemed prepared to work me to the bone, but he had made it clear on the drive there when I had tried to convince him otherwise that the matter was closed and there would be no further discussion about it.

"It's not quite boot camp," he said. "Still," and he smiled at Louise, "I'd rather be a guest here any day than to work for *you.*" He pushed his chair back from the table. "How's Lars?"

An odd name. It sounded like there were several of him.

Louise's face tightened and she stood up quickly to clear the dishes. "He's in Fargo on business for a few days. But he's the same," she said before she headed for the sink with the plates. "He still gets to play tennis coach with the guests—especially the ladies."

I rose to help her before she had to ask me, and to my surprise she said, "Not yet—I'll take care of these. Tomorrow's soon enough to start. Why don't you explore the place? There's a pond out back, and sixty acres of woods and fields. We'll get you settled into your room later."

I looked quickly at my father, knowing by his eyes that they wanted to talk by themselves, but I was afraid he would leave without saying good-bye.

"Go on, Rita—I'll be here a while yet."

I didn't want to go outside, didn't want to stay in either, so I went out the door but just stood there in the dirt drive by our station wagon. I laid my hand on the hood but it was so hot it stung and then I felt tears welling up as if my burned hand were finally a real reason to cry.

I didn't know what to do with myself. My body, full-grown already and as tall then as it would ever be, felt huge and heavy, though I was skinny by most people's standards. My hair hung in long hanks, straight and sweaty and stuck to my cheeks. Tears crawled down my face. Part of me wanted to fold up, just collapse and hug my knees in the backseat of the car, part of me wanted to run wild and blind down the hill.

The need to move was greater. I ran into unfamiliar terrain, made even stranger by my blurred sight, down an uneven, grassy slope to a small pond with a red rowboat tethered to a wooden dock. In the distance, I could see the Black Hills, but they looked green to me. There was something implacable about them and I liked it that they were there—something far away that seemed so close.

I walked out on the dock and stepped into the rowboat. The bottom of the pond was choked with weeds, and tadpoles wiggled from the banks to disappear in the murk and tangle. I liked being out on the water, but the pond was less than a hundred feet across and took a disappointingly short time to explore.

I tied the boat back to its iron ring at the dock and carefully folded the oars in like a pair of wings. Everything, I was sure, would have to pass muster. I walked slowly up the drive, breathing hard in the heat. My father was getting ready to leave and as he hugged me good-bye next to the station wagon I longed to get in there with him, prop my bare feet on the sun-warmed dashboard and spread the map across my legs. Hand him an opened bottle of Coke from the cooler when he asked for one. But he was going, and then he was gone, and I was left with Louise.

❖ Louise took me through every room in the house, beginning upstairs with the guest rooms. I was glad for the immediate distraction—there was so much to pay attention to. There were four-poster or brass beds in all the rooms, even a canopy in the honeymoon suite. There were braided, colorful rag rugs on the wooden floors, lace curtains in the windows, embroidered runners on the bureaus, Bibles on the nightstands.

Louise's own room was a mere cubbyhole beneath the stairs—windowless and close, with a severely slanted ceiling—the underside of the staircase that rose above her single bed. There was not even a picture on the wall. A bare wooden table held a stack of books: *Anna Karenina* and *Mythology of the American Indian*—books that looked like they'd take ages to read. The bedspread was tucked smooth and tight over the mattress, as if it had been ironed in place. Inside the doorless closet, several dresses and a winter coat hung stiffly on their hangers. I imagined her lying there in her narrow bed, listening to the pairs of footsteps falling above her on the stairs, waiting for a certain step to creak when they reached it.

My room was a second-story version of Louise's, except that it had windows and its ceiling slanted from the slope of the roof above it. It was right above the kitchen, its floor like an ear to the sounds of dishes being stacked, water nearly constant in the faucets.

Across the hall, she pointed out, was Lars's room. Through the open door I saw an enormous bedroom lined with south-facing windows. We didn't go in, just stood in the doorway for a second, and then she quickly moved down the stairs. I stuck my head in the door: a king-sized bed faced the windows. On the wall, a series of photographs I couldn't make out from where I stood. When I started for the stairs Louise was standing at the bottom, looking up at me. I felt like I'd been caught at something forbidden. Even though I couldn't see her face clearly, I could feel those blue eyes on me, could sense that white cloud in the iris like changing weather.

❖ For the first time in my life, I learned to get up at dawn. It turned out to be easier than I thought. The light was pretty then, the fields below my window a dark blond, and the hills truly black.

Louise steamed around the kitchen with a daunting energy. As far as I could tell, she never made mistakes. I made them with alarming frequency. I broke a juice glass more than once, never seemed to dry the dishes fast enough, and sliced the butter for the butter plates thicker than she wanted. Next to her thriftiness and vigor I felt extravagant and sloppy. She gave me neither praise nor scorn, she just told me exactly what she expected, which was a relief because it saved me from guessing, something I was used to at home. I thought of how my mother never made the bed, how she tossed her clothes over the backs of chairs as she stood frustrated in front of the mirror trying to decide what to wear before she went to town. The kitchen was a map of her indecision—things half-cooked or left to burn, a notepad by the phone crazy with scribblings and disconnected drawings. When I was in the fifth grade she decided to give me my birthday party at school. She was going to bring in enough cake and ice cream for the whole class. She rushed in a little late carrying a sheet cake in a pink box. She brought plastic forks and spoons. She seemed so confused and excited I didn't have the heart to tell her there were only nine candles on the cake instead of ten.

❖ The guests arrived in twos through that first Saturday morning. They all seemed young and in love and alternately bashful and bold around one another. The newlyweds stared dreamily at each other across their table by the window. I had to clear my throat to make them notice I was there and then they took a long time to make up their minds, as if love had crowded out their habits and preferences.

In contrast, a middle-aged couple that arrived on Sunday knew exactly what they wanted, down to the number of minutes and seconds for the boiling of their eggs.

I cleaned their rooms, using my passkey to let myself in. The newly-weds' room was dark, the shades pulled close, the sheets a tangle on the bed, the spread slipped down, heaped on the floor. In the bath-tub, both black hair and blond in the drain. Sweat and perfume stirred together in the air. On the nightstand, a tube of petroleum jelly, the cap off, the viscous stuff leaking onto the doily beneath it. Next to that, foil packages, one torn open. I knew right away what they were. I picked up one of the packages and placed it on the nightstand on the other side of the bed. I wanted them to know I'd been there. I felt a certain complicity with them, intimate with the smallest details of their honeymoon lives. I found myself hurrying through the break-fast dishes to get to the rooms, to look for the clues I believed they left behind because they wanted to tell me something, and when they smiled at me in the hallway or the dining room it seemed their secret was partly mine.

❖ One day after the lunch dishes were washed and put away Louise said, wiping her hands on her long apron, "I need some help out at the root cellar."

I followed her across the small field in back of the house through the wheat grass on either side of the worn path. She pointed out flowers along the way—prairie gentian and blazing star, coyote thistle and paintbrush. She had given me a wicker basket which I tried to carry on my head the way I'd seen African women do in *National Geographic,* but I had to hold on to it the whole time to keep it from falling off.

The root cellar was not really a cellar at all, but a quonset hut, a squat, curved building like a small airplane hangar. Louise opened the metal door at its end, then switched on her flashlight. We stepped inside. A cool, drafty darkness rushed at us, and Louise's light barely separated it. A dank, earthy smell closed around me. Louise shone the light on two wooden stools and a mound of something indistinguishable in front of them. She sat on one stool and held the light on the other for me. She balanced the flashlight on her lap to point in front of us and the mound took shape—a pile of potatoes, their eyes sprouting white, gnarled fingers.

"Just snap the sprouts off and toss the potatoes in the basket there." A pile of them was already accruing at her feet.

"It's so *dark,*" I said.

"It's not dark *enough.*" If she heard any fear in my voice she chose not to cater to it. She worked quickly, tossing the potatoes into a basket where they fell with a dull thud against each other.

I heard what I thought was thunder and then the rain followed almost immediately, amplified on the corrugated roof, sounding more like marbles than drops. We had enough potatoes by then, but Louise said, "We'll just wait until it blows over."

We didn't say anything for a time. The flashlight wavered and nearly went out until she slapped it hard in the palm of her hand, spanking it back to life. This happened several times.

Because it was dark and the rain took up the silence I braved a question.

"Did you ever have children?"

After a long pause she said, "I never did." She slapped the flashlight again.

"But did you want to?" I didn't think I was prying. My mother had always asked other women about their children —Avon ladies, Jehovah's Witnesses, women who came to our door. It seemed a question that women always came to with one another, and that helped them get along.

"Well I just couldn't have any, and not for lack of trying."

The flashlight dwindled to a glow little more than a candle flame and no amount of smacking would make it brighter.

The darkness seemed to press us closer though we didn't move at all. I thought I felt her sadness and knew that whatever had happened between her and Lars was bad enough to make a rift between them that widened over the years until they slept in opposite ends of the house.

I had to think about it hard before I did it, but I felt for her hand behind the flashlight, something I never would have done in broad daylight. She pulled her hand away as if I'd touched her by mistake. I was glad it was dark so she couldn't see my face, how quickly it changed from scared to surprised to shamed.

"Rain's stopped," she said.

❖ We walked back to the house with the basket of potatoes, the tall wet grass brushing against our pantcuffs, painting them a deeper, darker color than the legs. We were almost to the kitchen door when I heard a truck coming up the drive. Louise glanced down the road, then disappeared inside the house. It turned out to be not a truck but a jeep, and it pulled right up to the door. A tall man with blond hair just turning white swung his legs out and jumped down. I knew without having to be told that this was Lars.

"Well don't you look just like your mother."

I felt a small shock wave pass through me, as if my physical appearance had imitated her without my knowledge, that my face had allied itself somehow with the wrong side. He had to practically pick up my hand to shake it. I'd forgotten how.

"I'm Lars."

"I know," I said.

"I hope Lou isn't working you too hard—she's tough to keep up with sometimes."

His smile was friendly, his face held nothing I had to try to figure out. In spite of myself and in spite of Louise's anger toward him, I wanted to like him.

"Been fishing yet?" He didn't wait for an answer. "Well." He scratched his head in a parody of someone thinking. He opened the back of the jeep and pulled out a rod and reel, inspected it, tested its flex, then handed it to me. "I picked this up at a swap meet in Fargo. I thought you might be able to use it."

Just as he handed it to me I looked up and saw Louise framed in the screen door. She turned away as if she couldn't stand to watch. But it was too late—I couldn't just give it back. Besides, I wanted it. It was just a fishing pole, but it felt as heavy as a weapon in my hands.

❖ Lars ate supper with us but Louise managed not to speak directly to him unless she absolutely had to. She treated him like a paying guest, served up his meal without particular flourish or comment, her face blank as she ate. What passed between them were transactions—deliveries, grounds maintenance, the price of beef in town. I could only talk to one of them at a time. When I tried to thread us all together by asking a general question directed toward them both I could feel their stubborn refusal to confer. I thought of countless meals at home after one of my parents' arguments and how the sounds of chewing and the scrape of tines on unglazed plates became a din so loud it drowned out the words none of us could think of anyway.

❖ The next afternoon Lars wanted to take me down to the pond to try out my fishing rod. Louise let me go, but gave me a look that told me I was betraying her. She said she thought she'd go into town, knowing full well I would have liked to go too. I watched her car churn up the dust in the driveway—she couldn't get away fast enough.

Lars and I sat in the red rowboat and drifted with the prevailing breeze. We both wore hats to shade ourselves from the prairie sun and I trailed my left hand in the water. The pond, even in the middle, was swirling with weeds, and through those green tresses tadpoles skittered in a maze. If we drifted near the shore we heard a steady plopping rain as countless full-grown frogs launched themselves from the banks into the safety under water.

Lars showed me how to bait the hook—he had a dixie cup full of night crawlers—and how to cast the line. I liked the feeling of the line pulling out and the buzzing of the reel; I liked slowly coaxing it back to me again.

"Your mom and dad came up here on their honeymoon, you know."

"I know." Yet it felt strange hearing them coupled together in the same sentence, uttered by someone else, especially in reference to a time before I was even born.

"What room did they stay in?" I had to know.

"Well, let's see. As I recall, they were real disappointed the honeymoon suite was already taken, but they settled for the one across the hall—the one with the fireplace."

I knew that room. I'd cleaned every inch of it. I'd even found a silver dollar under the bed and kept it for myself. I tried to imagine my parents in that room, Louise listening to them climb the stairs over her and close the door. My mother—did she undress in the bathroom or right in front of my father? Were they shy with each other at first, did they swear they'd always be together from that night on? It struck me then that it was likely I was conceived in the very room I was tending to now. From where we drifted on the lake I could see its shuttered windows by the chimney, and then I wished they hadn't been there so long ago, that they were there now and would leave something of theirs behind in that room that I could find and keep.

The line jerked hard and I lost my balance. Lars reached over and just steadied me with his hand as I reeled it in.

"That's the girl. Nice and easy—you're doing fine." The words seemed to sink into me through the warmth of his palm on my shoulder. I wanted that fish, wanted to bring it out of that dark green water.

"Bluegill," he said as it broke the surface. He unhooked it and put it in the yellow bucket of water behind me in the bow. It wiggled, it thrashed and tried to jump out. I couldn't stand it—I poured it back into the pond and watched it slip into the weeds and disappear.

I looked at Lars quickly, ready to be scolded or laughed at.

"What the hell," he said. "It's good luck to let the little ones go anyhow." He wiped the back of his neck with a bandana. "Ready for a sandwich yet?"

I reached into the cooler and handed him a ham sandwich wrapped in an envelope of waxed paper. I thought about Louise neatly tucking in the ends.

"Did Louise ever come fishing with you?"

He looked up at the house as if its presence there might help him remember. "I can't say that she ever did."

"Did you ever do *any*thing together?"

The blazing heat and being away from land were making me bolder than I usually felt.

"You notice a lot in a short time. Eagle eye, aren't you?" He didn't say anything for a minute. He seemed to be studying his hands. Then he looked at the fields, the line of fir trees at their edges.

"We used to walk these sixty acres. She knew every inch of it —she could tell from one year to the next exactly where the wildflowers would show."

I thought of my mother, who did not know the names of flowers and couldn't tell one bird from another, who looked at me sometimes in a way that made me think she'd forgotten who I was and why I was living in her house.

Lars seemed lost in the idea of Louise he had conjured up, and as he turned his gaze toward the grassy slope rising from the pond I tried to imagine the two of them. It was hard to picture Lars next to her—would he have stood close, touched her shoulder? I had no trouble seeing Louise. She was gathering black-eyed susans and prairie roses, the sap staining her fingers green, the white blood of milkweed flowing where they'd passed.

❖ On Wednesdays Louise gave instruction in *Menzendieck*, a German form of physical therapy. Her "classes" were one-on-one—two or three regulars back to back in the afternoon down at the barn. She never would tell me much about it and I was curious, so one Wednesday I hid in the tall weeds by the side of the barn and watched through a chink between the worn red-gray boards. Louise's client, a Mrs. Caulfield, was newly married and concerned that her chronic back pain would give her difficulty in carrying a child. This I heard easily—I was breathing not five feet from where they spoke. Louise told her to undress in the tack room—"Everything but your panties"—and that there were hangers for her clothes.

Mrs. Caulfield came back out in her loafers and hip-high underpants. Her breasts shook as she walked. Louise said, "Now then," and steered her in front of three large mirrors, the two at the sides slightly angled for a more complete side and back view like the ones in dressing rooms at department stores. They stood in that bright circumference, their reflections tripled, the light from the hayloft window glancing off the reflective surface. Tiny motes of hay dust hung suspended like hundreds of tiny spiders spinning on the ends of threads. Louise put her hands on the woman's narrow hips—I thought for sure they were going to dance. But Louise simply turned the woman to face herself in the mirror, then turned her slowly to the side.

"Stand the way you normally do."

The woman's body changed right then and there. Her pelvis tipped forward, her stomach slouched, her spine curved like a question mark, her knees locked.

"Now take a good look at yourself." The woman turned her head to view the triptych of her body in the mirrors.

"Do you see?" Louise's voice was soft, encouraging. I had thought she would take on the role of a drill sergeant, whip that woman into shape by pointing out her flaws. But Louise cupped her fingers beneath the woman's chin as if she might kiss her and lifted Mrs. Caulfield's head until her back straightened.

"Now, think of a point just above the top of your head, and raise your body up to meet it."

Mrs. Caulfield's body actually grew taller as if it had always been caught and bunched up and suddenly allowed to unfurl.

"Now look again."

Mrs. Caulfield turned her head toward her new reflection and stared as if she didn't recognize herself. I thought she was going to cry.

"I didn't realize . . . "

"People never do. Some are stiff as ramrods, others just slouch as if they're ashamed. Either way, over time it molds the muscles. It's a matter now of remolding. Now—walk over to that thresher and back again and keep in mind that sense of your body rising to meet that place just above your head."

Mrs. Caulfield started out stiff, but by the time she got to the thresher she was fairly gliding across the floor. She stopped there after she turned around, just stood there for a second, and her body, the white roundness of her breasts, seemed so incongruously soft next to the rusted metal with its sharp edges and massive, silent bulk. Her body seemed small and flat—hardly big enough for a child to ever fit inside her, her breasts not big enough to feed anyone for very long. I realized I had never seen my mother's body naked, that I couldn't even imagine her face anymore though it had only been three weeks since she'd gone. When I tried to remember her voice, it wouldn't come to me. I was scared that I'd forgotten her without meaning to, and knew then that I could be misplaced inside my mother's mind. I wanted to cry but didn't dare make a sound for fear I'd be discovered. Mrs. Caulfield walked back to Louise, but the two of them were blurred now, blurred together through a hot, embarrassing flow of silent tears. Louise stood behind her, I think, and it seemed they raised their arms together like two birds with a single pair of wings.

❖ Louise was scrubbing potatoes under a steady stream of water in the sink. She heard me come in—I'd just finished cleaning the guest rooms. It was Monday, a slow day even in summer.

"Give Lars's room a cleaning today if you're done with the other rooms."

She went on furiously scrubbing the red skins on the new potatoes—they seemed flushed somehow from her efforts. I couldn't see her face but I could feel, just by the way she said "Lars's room," that it was a place she wouldn't set foot in, even to sweep it clean.

I dragged the Electrolux up the back stairs, down the narrow hallway between his room and mine. I used the outlet in the hall and I had to give the retractable cord a good yank so it wouldn't go snaking back inside again. When I opened the door, the light was nearly blinding from the afternoon sun in all those south-facing windows, the double bed neatly made. It was so still in there I could hear a small bee outside bumping against the windowpane. Dust hung in the shafts of streaming light, neither rising nor falling. I moved closer to the row of sepia photographs that hung on the wall by the bed. At first all I saw was a grassy hill, a fleece of clouds rising behind it, then I leaned in closer. There was a man lying prone on the hill, naked, his face turned away from the camera, turned to watch the clouds coming toward him. In the next photograph, the man was standing, his back curved against a cottonwood tree. His right leg was raised, knee bent, the sole of his foot braced against the trunk behind him, not completely hiding his genitals. His arms were raised over his head, his head thrown back, his hands pressed flat against the tree behind him. It seemed his entire body curved against that tree.

In the third, a close-up of just his face. His eyes were closed. I knew it was Lars, though he was at least twenty years younger that day when the person with the camera asked him to do these things. Blades of grass grazed his ears—he looked as if he'd grown from the ground he was lying on.

In the fourth, his eyes were open, and in the dark center of the pupils, the reflected clouds; around his head, like a dark aura, the shadow of someone leaning over him.

I lifted the picture from the wall. A rectangle of a paler color hung below the nail. I looked close at the bottom of the right-hand corner of the print to see if I could make out what was written there—Louise, 1943.

I put it back. I sat down on the edge of the bed. Their bed. I turned around and pulled back the covers and sheets. The side nearest the nightstand with the books on it held a shape—a certain pressure on the ticking over the years, the tall imprint of a man. The other side, smooth as new snow on an outdoor table. I ran my hand across it—not a trace where her hip must have once pressed into the mattress. I lay down and spread my arms wide across the cool white expanse and still my outstretched fingers didn't reach to either end.

I remembered my parents' bed, how it was small, nearly concave in the middle like a bowl, and how they must have rolled toward each other in sleep. Now my father would fall into it every night alone.

I made the bed and smoothed the covers. There was no evidence that I'd been there and unmade it, and stared. I dusted and cleaned, I set it right, welcoming her back like a woman long away who's bound to come home.

❖ "Mail's come. Letter for you, Rita." Louise didn't raise her head from doing her accounts at the table. A white envelope lay on the dark, scoured countertop. I slid my finger in at the end and ripped it open. There was no return address, but I'd know my father's hand anywhere. Besides, the postmark said San Francisco. So he made it there. There was a short note from him, hoping I was working hard and getting rich. He said he was enclosing a letter to me from my mother that she had asked him to forward. I just stared at it, afraid to open it. I'd never had a letter from her before, never been that far away to have to be written to.

The paper was pink and smelled like a purple flower.

> *Dear Rita,*
>
> *I suppose Daddy told you I'm staying at Aunt Kate's in San Francisco. It seems so strange to be near the ocean! (Lake Michigan is nothing like it, believe me.) I'll probably be here for at least the rest of the summer. After that, I don't know.*
>
> *That day I left—you were still at school—I drove back by the house in a taxi when I knew you'd be getting home just so I could see you. You were sitting on the porch steps with Susan Fineman. The cab slowed—did you notice? I intended to stop, but then I didn't know what to say. But Rita, I want to tell you your hair looked so nice that day and all of a sudden you seemed so grown up to me.*
>
> *With Love,*
> *Mom*

"Everything all right at home now?" Louise was looking at me over the half-glasses she wore for her accounts. She looked almost kind and I wanted to answer, but all I could do was just shrug and push my way out the screen door. I stuffed the letter in my jeans pocket and headed for the pond.

I heard the soft *pock, pock* of tennis balls on the court. Lars was teaching a young couple from St. Paul how to serve. I didn't stop to watch.

I dragged the boat off the bank where it was turned over to dry out and pushed it into the water. I pulled the oars in after me, slammed the pins into the oarlocks, and rowed hard, but the pond's diameter wasn't wide enough to put any real distance between myself and the shore. I just drifted for a while. I leaned over the side and watched the tadpoles wriggle in the muddy shallows. They were nearly frogs, about to burst their tails. They looked stupid and helpless and I couldn't stand looking at them anymore. She wasn't even thinking about coming back, and my father, for all his driving toward her, was no closer than when he left. I pulled an oar out of the lock, clenched both hands around the middle, the paddle like a blade pointed down, and I stabbed into the water in a blind rage. Again and again I brought the paddle down, trying to kill as many as I could. My clothes were soaking wet in minutes, muddy water stung my eyes. The boat pitched wildly and I nearly fell in. And then, after what felt like forever, I stopped as suddenly as I had begun. I let the oar slip into the water and drift away. I didn't even try to retrieve it. I just lay down in the bottom of the boat. I opened my mouth, stunned by the word that came out. "Louise," I cried.

❖ When I served dinner to a family of six that night, only five dinners made it in front of the guests. I had completely forgotten to serve the father. Most surprising of all, he didn't get mad, just politely waved me down when I went past to serve another couple their coffee. He said, "I think you forgot me," and smiled. I must have turned five shades of red. Afterward, when they'd gone and I came in to clear up, there was a five-dollar bill tucked beneath his plate.

Lars went up to his room after dinner to read. Louise and I washed the dishes and then we sat down to "Wagon Train" in the TV lounge. The guests had all gone into town for a movie—*Barefoot in the Park*—so we had the place to ourselves.

Louise disappeared for a few minutes. I heard her clattering around in the kitchen, then the sound of popcorn ricocheting off the lid of a pan. She came back bearing a large wooden bowl full of popcorn.

There was even butter on it. She was trying to be kind—maybe she'd guessed about the letter. We placed the bowl on the couch between us. She ate with her left hand, I ate with my right. We watched.

Ward Bond was lost. The horses had stampeded in a flash flood and he went after them and got thrown. He was up to his neck in water and drowning. Then an Indian girl found him, held a long branch out to him from the riverbank. She pulled him out and laid him on the grass until his eyes opened. You could tell when he finally came to he thought he was in a dream.

The lights flickered just then, and above the sound of the storm on television we could hear the storm beginning just outside. Louise jumped up and turned the TV off—the program wasn't even finished yet. "Lightning could ruin the tube," she explained. She walked over and stood in front of the picture window. It was nearly dark, the clouds near the horizon an inky black and a slash of red where the sun had just gone down. Lightning flashed, then Louise counted five till thunder.

"It's still a ways off," she said, turning toward me. She turned to the window again. "God, we could use this rain."

She seemed to be thinking hard about something as she stood there, as if she was summoning the rain, willing it to come. I couldn't take my eyes off her. And then she turned to me again with the oddest smile.

"Come on," she said.

She headed for the door. Once off the porch steps she began to run, and I had to move fast not to lose her. We stopped at the gate to the south field. She yanked the laces on her shoes.

"The shoes have to go," she said.

I pulled off my sneakers—we left them by the gate—then we ran into the field. It was dry and windy and the clouds seemed to glow as if reflecting the light of a vast city beneath them. The field hadn't been mowed in some time—the buffalo and wheat grass came to our knees, and there was no short stubble to cut our feet. Lightning exposed the woods at the edges, the cumulus towered above. The wind was rising fast. Louise's hair came partly undone from its knot. I was almost afraid as I ran, but I felt wild and excited too, coming so close to danger with permission.

We stopped in the middle of the field, doubled over to catch our breath. Louise gasped for air and started to laugh—it startled me because I couldn't remember hearing her laugh before. She headed toward the woods. I stayed right behind her.

At the edge of the woods the trees grew so tall and close together the wind didn't find us, just moaned in the topmost boughs. A twig snapped beneath my foot and she turned around sharply, her finger held to her lips.

"This is how Indians walk, without a sound."

It was so dark in those woods I could barely see her except, when the lightning flared, in a freeze-frame of motion, her arms out for balance, her foot poised in midair like a dancer's.

"Step down just on the ball of your foot, then slowly lower the rest of your foot till your heel touches down."

I did as she asked, walked behind her with as much stealth as I could manage.

"That's right—you've got the idea."

I felt warm inside, encouraged. We walked that way, like Indians, along the tree line.

I followed her back into the field and we stopped in sight of the house. I could see a light come on in Lars's window. The rain poured out of the sky all at once—no scattered drops preceded it. We were drenched in less than a minute and when lightning came again I could see each detail clearly for half a second, sometimes a little longer—her shirt soaked through, transparent, the outline of her breasts, her white hair undone, long and wet and curling at the ends. Her pants rolled up to her knees, her calves slick with the strokes of rain-soaked grass. She took my hand and we just stood there for a time. I didn't move for fear I'd break the spell, that she'd let go again.

"I'll teach you how to dance."

She shifted her feet just slightly, put one hand on my shoulder, held the other out into the wind.

"Don't look at your feet—just follow."

I came inside the half-circle her body made and she put her other arm around me.

We danced slowly, flattening out a small space in the wall of grass. Over her shoulder, I saw Lars coming, trudging through the field. He stopped when he saw us, stood completely still, transfixed, and didn't come any closer. I believe she knew he was there, that she wanted him to see that she could still dance without him.

Louise danced for rain, asked it right down from that Dakota sky. I began to feel as fluid as the grass that moved in waves around us. I did not stumble. I danced for what I hoped I could bring back to me, for what I knew or guessed of love.

❖ *About the Author*

Photo: Michael Lauchlan

"The desire to write is the one point that never shifts, a point I can return to again and again like a section marker planted firmly in a wild, eroding terrain. The people in my stories, if they could say it right out loud, would tell you about the eerie, beautiful moment of grace under pressure. Instead, they slip me notes and I write it down. Their stories are the breathing spaces in a headlong rush to be heard."

Alison Moore received an M.F.A. in creative writing from Warren Wilson College in 1990. She lives in Tucson, where she teaches fiction at Pima College and for the Tucson Writers' Project. She is also the administrative director of ArtsReach, a nonprofit organization dedicated to teaching creative writing to native American children. "Leaving by the Window" won the Martindale Literary Prize in Arizona.